The Snowflake Inn

A CHRISTMAS NOVELLA

MELISSA JEAN

TABLE OF CONTENTS

Chapter 1

CHRISTMAS TIME.

My most favourite time of the year. So much so, that every year I buy a special advent calendar starting November first, allowing me to enjoy an extended festive countdown right up until the very day. And Christmas, is the exact reason I'm in this mess right now.

Snowed in and unable to go anywhere.

I glance out the window, watching the snow fall in heavy sheets as the wind howls, shaking the trees violently.

Only half an hour ago, the sweet owners of this adorable inn, Pearl and Dusty, called all the guests into the festive, yet tastefully themed living room, to tell us that the roads were blanketed in snow and we were unable to leave.

For the foreseeable future anyway.

The road into my childhood hometown where my parents still live, is also snowed in and not accessible. Thankfully, my plans aren't to be there for another week anyway, so panic hasn't set in just yet.

The other vacationers were mostly unfussed, but one was downright angry. As if Pearl and Dusty had some kind of control over the weather.

The inn has six rooms, five of which are currently occupied.

There's myself, three older couples who are just warm and wonderful and who are all vacationing together, and a man named Sawyer, who looks to be roughly late thirties like me, and who has me puzzled as to why he even booked this place to begin with.

He seems to genuinely dislike Christmas and has done nothing but complain since he arrived. The inn is too 'Christmasy' for his liking.

The description of the inn says: *Festive themed Christmas inn. Each room is adorned in decorative items to allow for an immersive Christmas experience. All meals and music are Christmas themed.*

I tuned out his complaints over breakfast this morning and thankfully he has kept to his room ever since.

The inn is the definition of Christmas. Pearl and Dusty, the owners of the inn, have been bringing Christmas joy to their guests since they opened, forty years ago.

As a Christmas lover, The Snowflake Inn is everything I could have hoped for and more.

I've driven past this inn with my family since I was a kid, and then as a teen and an adult. The online pictures do not do it justice.

It's a white two storey, large cottage style inn with white shutters and a wraparound verandah. Christmas tunes play softly from speakers in each of the common rooms, and the smell of pine needles, hot cider and warm sugar cookies all waft from the kitchen, filling the inn. Real garlands and wreaths adorn mantels, doors, tables and bookshelves. Tasteful red ribbons are strategically placed around the rooms. Not a single piece of plastic tinsel or cheap decoration is in sight. It is clear that a lot of love and time has been put into this place.

Twinkly delicate lights also strung in each room, invite a sense of cosiness. A sign on the front lawn explains that the inn was originally built in 1885 and it has been carefully restored. The original exposed wooden beams, extend across the ceilings of the kitchen, and plush, soft rugs cover the floors in each room. A brick and stone fireplace, is the centrepiece for the living room downstairs and arched doorways and intricate cornices feature in each room.

The bedrooms have the same finer details and are situated on the top floor. I can't attest to the other rooms, but my own bathroom has a claw foot bathtub. As soon as I had checked into my room and unpacked, I ran a bubble bath and relaxed in the warm soapy water, the scent of orange and cinnamon bath crystals filling the air. I was so relaxed, I had closed my eyes for a moment, slipping further under the water, exhaling loudly. I can't wait to run another bath tonight.

This place is truly a Christmas wonderland.

I've missed the last two Christmas' with my family, and there was no way I was going to allow a third. My grand plan had been to stay at The Snowflake Inn and take in the sights of this cute little town for the next week, before driving the thirty minutes over to the next town, where my parents live. I planned to surprise them on Christmas Eve for their annual, Christmas extravaganza.

It all started when I was a baby, and with me being the oldest, it has continued every year.

During our Christmas extravaganza, my parents outdo themselves ever year. My brother, sister and I come together in a flurry of Christmas eve gimmicky gifts, Christmas movies, hot chocolate and night sky watching, for Santa. We might not believe in Santa anymore, but the best part of the evening, is us all sitting on the verandah by the outdoor fireplace, and star gazing over a steaming mug of apple cider.

I've missed it so much.

All thanks to Felix.

Although really, it's my fault I stayed with him so long.

He hated Christmas and refused to go home and see my family. And that should have been warning enough that he wasn't worth my time.

It took me two whole years of him ignoring me in place of his 'buddies' and his job, to finally say goodbye. I felt lighter the minute I did, which speaks volumes.

The day I broke it off with him, I went straight to my favourite café and treated myself to an iced coffee and chocolate muffin, before jumping on their Wi-Fi and booking this trip.

And my family have no idea.

Only a few days ago I spun a story to them about being so busy with work that I couldn't leave, once again unable to make Christmas. I felt guilty only for a few moments when I heard the disappointment in their voices, but it will all be worth it when I ring that doorbell. I can practically smell my mum's famous Christmas pudding.

Excitement bubbles in my stomach, just thinking about my week ahead and surprising my family.

A pang hits my chest when I remember that we are snowed in.

I send out a silent prayer that the snow clears right in time for Christmas eve.

So, I'm sitting here, by the crackling, warm fireplace, in what must be the happiest inn on Earth, enjoying a hot chocolate and reading my book, when I hear the front door swing open and quickly close. Pearl and Dusty, call out, greeting their next guest.

I'm surprised to hear that someone else has arrived, knowing that we are now snowed in. Whoever it is, must have been on their way here and just snuck through as the roads closed.

I can hear a man's voice, and guess that he must be asking if there's any vacancies. Hopefully he has more Christmas cheer than Sawyer.

"Yes, we have one room left dear," Pearl replies in her soft, sweet voice.

Interesting.

They mustn't have planned on staying here but have gotten snowed in like the rest of us.

A deep voice speaks quietly, too softly for me to really make out anything, and I can't explain why, but a shiver slices through me.

Curiosity gets the better of me and I stand, grabbing my drink, waving goodbye to the other guests chatting at the tables. I'm keen to see who our newest guest is. Their room will be right next to mine at the end of the hall, and I pray it's not another Sawyer. I don't do well with confrontation, and he makes me nervous enough.

Thankfully Sawyer is in his room, or he would find a way to complain about someone new being here. When I greeted him yesterday, he stared at me silently, analysing me, and then point blank told me I look just like a television star he finds really irritating.

I glance at the mirror as I walk past it and know exactly which actor he is speaking of. I've been told that for years, but never with such contempt or irritation.

My long blonde hair falls in waves, trailing halfway down my back, just like said actor and my blue green eyes have been compared to tropical waters, very similar to hers too. My lips are full naturally and my nose turns up a little at the end.

It is actually uncanny how similar the television star Petra Simco and I look, even down to our athletic body shape. Finding outfits that give my straight up and down shape more curves was always tricky, and I worried way too much about that as a teen. I just stopped caring the older I got and started wearing whatever the hell I wanted and somehow it works.

I'm in one of my favourite outfits currently, a white fitted tee tucked into my favourite ankle length frayed denims with a cute brown sandal. It's so toasty warm at the inn that I don't even need a cardigan.

I step into the small entrance room, planning on saying a quick hi to my new, temporary neighbour, before taking my hot chocolate upstairs to catch up on some more reading.

Although I enjoy being around people sometimes, my favourite place to be, is lost in pages.

I push down my nerves, never very good at social interactions and plaster what I hope, looks like a warm smile to welcome them. I glance up quickly, a soft hello leaving my lips, before all the air is sucked out of my lungs.

"Asher?" I whisper, my voice edging on disbelief, my heart all but pounding out of my chest.

The man standing by the door talking to Pearl, whips his head in my direction, his eyes shooting towards mine, his mouth dropping open in surprise.

"Cassidy? What are you doing here?" He asks in that deep, timbre tone.

I can't quite find the words for the man standing in front of me.

Asher Mills. Famous rockstar and frontman for Ash & Stone.

And my first love.

Chapter 2

THE ROOM IS SILENT BEFORE someone clears their throat. Pearl, I think, but I'm too stunned to pay attention.

"Oh, do you two know each other? Isn't that a wonderful surprise. I guess we don't need to tell you that Mr Mills is very famous, and we must keep it a secret he is here. I best be off to let everyone else know," Pearl says before taking off to notify the other guests.

Dusty picks up Asher's bag and says in his raspy voice, "I'll get this up to your room for you, young man. You're in room six, right next to Cassidy here. You both share a beautiful view of the back garden and the woodlands behind. We get foxes and deer that come up to the fence too. Right then, off I go."

Dusty hikes up the stairs whistling a tune. They really are the happiest people I've ever met.

It's Ashers turn to clear his throat. His eyes dart across my face before doing a quick sweep down and back up.

"Cassidy… wow it's been a long time. Seventeen years actually. You look… good. Amazing, actually."

I exhale loudly and I wish there was a hole around that could swallow me up. My whole life, I've always been someone who was labelled 'shy' and I've hated it but was always too uncomfortable to correct people. Hence the label.

Asher would remember me that way, although with him, I always felt free to be myself. Over the years, I've worked really hard to try and be more outgoing, and less of a people pleaser.

I give him a warm smile, determined to not let this reunion shake my confidence. My relationship with Asher was one of those fiery, passionate ones, where we had our future mapped out after only a few weeks together.

He was the cliche 'one that got away'.

We dated for six years, from sixteen till I was twenty-two before we broke up. It was an amicable break up and my biggest regret in life.

And now he's standing in front of me, looking better than he should.

He was always good looking, in a cute way. He was everyone's crush when we were younger.

But now? He's everyone's wet dream. On stage and TV and now I can attest to in person too.

Rocks hottest front man and a regular feature in my own dreams.

He's tall at 6 foot 4, with caramel coloured hair in that rockstar, hairstyle. Shorter on the sides and longer on the top.

His dark green eyes are still the same, but more intense somehow. His jeans, boots, tee and black leather jacket are unable to hide the strong body beneath, and I'm privy to what's under there from his recent photoshoot for Rock Mag. I secretly bought two copies, in case I lost one.

I didn't think it was even possible to be that toned and have muscles like that, but I can see in real life, none of it was photoshopped. I realise then I've been standing here in silence, staring at him for way too long.

"Umm, yeah seventeen years. Has it been that long? Wow. You look really good too… how have you been Asher?" I ramble nervously. I know exactly how long it's been, and I have no idea why I said that.

It's a loaded question and I regret asking it as soon as it slips from my mouth. There's no way to summarise seventeen years into a 'Good thanks and you?'.

He stares at me, doing his own appraising of me. He places his hands on his head, his shirt lifting a little at the front. Yep, definitely not photoshopped.

"I'm good… I just can't believe you're here Cassidy. I mean what are the chances?"

I shrug uncomfortably, still feeling rattled by him being here.

"It sounded like you weren't meant to be here? From what Pearl said earlier, I mean."

He shakes his head, lowering his hands to his waist.

"I had a break in touring, and I wanted to head home for Christmas. I got as far as the highway before I was turned back. I figured I was so close, I may as well see if there was anything around that was open. Not even twenty minutes later, they closed the road out. And here I am."

He gives me that cheeky, cocky smile. The one that fans all over the world go wild for.

The one I always went wild for. He pulls off that arrogant look because he's always just been a good guy underneath it all.

"Well, I'm glad you're here… it's nice to see you Asher," I tell him quietly and truthfully.

His smile turns soft, and he tilts his head to the side. "It's nice to see you too Peaches."

I blush at his use of my nickname. The name, only he had for me.

He always said when I would blush, my cheeks reminded him of a peach and the name stuck. I've not heard it in seventeen years.

I awkwardly gesture towards the stairs. "I'll let you get settled in. I'm going to head to my own room, for a little while before dinner."

Wait, did that sound like I thought he might want me, to go to his room?

"I mean, not like I would be going to anyone else's room. Or expect to. I don't expect to. Just my own. Okay, I'm going now. To my room," I all but squeak, desperate to get out of here. In my rush to escape, I fumble my book, almost losing it and my hot drink in the process.

I point at the stairs, begore giving him an awkward little wave, making my way hurriedly to the staircase. I can feel the hot flush spreading all over my face, chest and neck.

Argh, play it cool Cassidy.

I take the first few steps, before realising he is following behind me. I hear him clearing his throat and I glance down over my shoulder to find him staring at my butt.

I thank earlier me who put on my nice jeans today, even though I wasn't going anywhere.

From the look on his face, it certainly looks like my pants choice is being appreciated.

His eyes meet mine and he laughs, clearly amused. He holds his hands up, in surrender. "Busted, and I'm not at all embarrassed about it either."

I keep my expression neutral before I turn back to face the stairs, a small grin spreading across my face. When we reach the top of the stairs, I feel an overwhelming urge to break the silence and point to the left "Right this way sir," I jokingly add, and he follows me along, moving to walk by my side.

It's a small corridor so we don't get far, before I stop in front my door.

"Well, this is me. I'll see you soon." I duck my head and turn the handle before Asher's hand reaches out to cover mine.

"Hey," he says softly. "It really is good to see you. I've missed you, Peaches."

Oh. I didn't expect that.

My heart is pounding, and I inhale deeply, trying to calm it.

"I've missed you too, Asher." I slide my fingers off the door handle, and he lets go, stepping back. We share a smile before I duck my head again, stepping into the room and closing the door.

Only when the door is finally closed, do I let out the breath I've been holding in.

Chapter 3

I DID NOT READ AT all. Not even a sentence of my book.

Instead, I spent the rest of the afternoon picking up my book only to lay it back down.

To then pace across the room, to then pick it back up before throwing it, and myself, onto the bed.

This little back and forth charade continued for about an hour.

What is he even doing here? And what are the chances that we are both here, at the exact same time.

I can hardly believe it.

I groan into my pillow.

I'm a mess. An emotional, giddy mess.

I can't decide if I'm excited, scared, nervous or freaking out.

A mix of all the above, would be accurate.

And to make matters worse, I can hear him softly strumming a guitar next door.

I go into absolute fan mode and sit in the chair closest to the wall we share, resting my cheek against the cool smooth surface, ear pressed as close as I can. I can hear him softly singing too, but it's not a song I've ever heard.

It's beautiful and not like any of the music he normally sings.

It's slow and soft and his voice croons as he hits the chorus, an ache echoing in his voice.

I could listen all day.

I stay in that seat for longer than I would ever admit, unable to quite make out the words, but his voice and the longing in it, settles into my heart.

I've missed him every day of those seventeen years. The day I left was the hardest of my life.

And every relationship since that one, has been compared to the one I had with him. The gold standard for every relationship I've ever had. Even when I didn't mean to.

I've followed his rise to fame all these years, and I am so unbelievably proud of him.

But every awards night attended with someone else, or the pictures taken with other women, was like a dagger to my heart. One small comfort, although a very tiny one at that, was knowing I wasn't cut out for the life he lives.

In the public eye all the time, with no privacy.

The thought of being in the public eye makes me cringe and a hot flush takes over my entire body, just thinking about it. Though funnily enough, I've had to present about my research and projects, at large conferences regularly and I do so without a single bead of sweat. There's something to be said about being in front of people for the work you do, rather than being under scrutiny, for you as a person or because of your association with someone.

But in spite of knowing I couldn't do that life, all those feelings are still there just bubbling under the surface, rushing back, the moment I saw him again in the flesh. They always have been, and I've known that for seventeen years, but before I could at least keep them at bay.

Not now it seems, and that means something. I know it does.

Could he feel the same? That same electrical pull.

A sharp ache hits my chest at the thought, and I dismiss it almost instantly, because it's incredibly unlikely that he would after all this time. Especially considering the incredible women he has worked with and met over the years.

I've mentally kept track of each of them, to my own detriment.

Maybe that spark is still so strong for me because I've been following his progress for years and he hasn't seen or heard of me in all that time.

Another thought occurs to me, striking me hard in the chest. He might be dating someone.

My heart lurches at the thought.

His photo shoot with Rock Mag this year not only included some very orgasm worthy pictures but also featured a Q&A section.

I gobbled up his answers like a starved little mouse.

They asked him about his favourite hobbies, and I got all warm and fuzzy when he told them that other than song writing, he loves to paint.

Not long after we started dating, I planned a date night for us, and it included dinner and a couples art class. We laughed so hard that night and my art was terrible, but Asher was really good. I shouldn't have been so surprised, he is a creative and artistic genius.

We continued to go to couples' art classes right up until our relationship ended, so it was a nice surprise to read that he still enjoys painting.

The rest of the article was them looking for straight up gossip.

He was direct when they asked if he is in a relationship.

His response? *'No, I don't have time'.*

Unless that's changed recently, I'm hoping it's still the same answer.

I roll onto my back, groaning, covering my eyes.

"Argh, what am I doing? There's no point to any of this anyway. We will see each other for a few days until the snow clears and then we go our separate ways. And before I know it, it will be another seventeen years before we see each other again," I mutter to myself, hoping that by saying it out loud, I'll develop some common sense here.

I sit up and reach for my open suitcase, searching through for a nice dress that I can wear to dinner. Nothing too fancy but still cute.

Score. I pull out my favourite dress. It's a coffee brown, button down dress with narrow straps and a small frill on the edge, that sits over my shoulders. It cuts in at the waist, giving the illusion that I have some shape at my hips and reaches mid-way down my calf.

It's perfect. It gives, 'not trying too hard, but also cute'. I pair it with a super soft cream cardigan.

I step into the dress and drape the cardigan over my arm. I quickly brush out my hair, before slipping my feet into brown flats. One of the great parts about being at the inn, is that I can dress in whatever I like because the place is on a set temperature.

And between that and the fireplace downstairs, I'm more than toasty right now, even with sub zero temperatures outside.

I'm too busy thinking about seeing Asher downstairs, that when I open my door and step out, I don't even see him standing there, his hand raised to knock.

I slam into him, surprising us both and knocking him backwards. I go flying with him.

He stumbles back before hitting the floor and I land right on top of him, my chin crashing into his hard chest. I lay my palms down beside his chest, pushing myself up slightly, my eyes meeting his.

Asher's eyebrows shoot up and he has an amused expression on his face, his perfect lips curling into a laughing grin.

"I mean, I'll never complain about being in this position Peaches but next time maybe just proposition me like a normal person," he says with that playful smirk.

I giggle and close my eyes, my face dropping back to his chest in embarrassment.

His finger curls under my chin and he lifts it back up. "Hey… you don't ever have to be embarrassed with me Cass. Ever, okay?" His tone is my undoing, just as much as his words.

His voice sounds like liquid honey pouring over me and I nod, giving him a small, reserved smile.

I sit up again, landing heavily on my butt. I reach out my hand to help him sit up. He chuckles, taking my hand and sitting up.

I didn't realise when I put out my hand to help him, that he would be sitting so close to me once he was upright.

Our faces are so close, I can feel his breath tickling my lips. His breathing is a little shallow, and I realise mine is too. He's as affected as I am. His hand reaches out and tucks my hair behind my ear, his fingers trailing down my jaw and neck, landing on my collarbone.

I inhale sharply at his touch, before scrambling backwards to stand.

My voice is hoarse and croaky when I speak, and I'm rewarded with another of his beautiful smiles.

"Umm we don't want to be late for dinner. Shall we head down?" He stands, stepping back a little, giving me some space this time. "Sure Peaches, lead the way."

Chapter 4

We only take a few steps down the hall when his phone rings.

A flash of irritation crosses his face when he looks at the screen, but he answers so quickly that I can't make out the name of the caller. He answers the phone in a gruff tone. Curiosity gets the better of me and I pull out my phone, trying to look like I'm not listening, when I absolutely am.

He listens for a few moments before groaning and running his hands over his face. I can only hear one side of the conversation, but he doesn't sound impressed when he finally speaks.

"I asked to not be disturbed for this week Elle. Just one week of no work talk." He listens to whatever Elle has to say in response and I take a guess that she is his manager. He taps his foot on the carpet and even that act of frustration, is rhythmic coming from him.

He looks at me and mouths "Sorry" and then, "I'll only be a minute" which I take to mean, he wants me to wait.

I pop my phone back into my pocket and don't even bother trying to hide the fact that I'm listening. He asked me to wait and it's a quiet hallway, so I kind of don't have a choice anyway.

His foot suddenly stops tapping.

"I'm sorry, what did you say?" He sounds confused and a little in disbelief.

He shakes his head at whatever he hears. "That's ridiculous. Don't people have anything better to do at this time of the year?"

He murmurs a few more non-committal responses and thanks the caller before ending the call.

He sighs and when I turn to face him, and I notice he looks weary and tired.

"Are you okay?"

He takes the last two steps to reach the staircase and sits down on the top step, his arms resting on his legs. "Yeah, just tired. This tour has really kicked my butt. It's been the best tour I've ever done, and I've enjoyed it, but I've not had a break in a year. I told my manager I wanted the week off leading into Christmas and to not call, but that was her."

I step down, taking a seat beside him, tucking my hands into my skirt on my lap.

I didn't notice it before, but I do now. He sounds tired.

"She rang to tell me that my fans have been trying to find out where I am. We did a press release a week ago to say I was vacationing, and now they are on the hunt to work out where."

My brows furrow at that, slightly alarmed at his words.

"That's awful Asher, and a total invasion of your privacy."

"Yep. Someone on socials has put out a campaign, asking for people to keep an eye out for me and if anyone spots me, to post a picture of my location with the hashtag 'foundashermills'."

I sit in shock, at a loss for words. His shoulders sink in a little he turns his head to face mine, giving me a weak smile that doesn't meet his eyes. Suddenly, I feel very protective of him, and I want to do something drastic. Like pick a location in another country and tag him being there, just to redirect their search.

"Asher… that's kind of scary."

He sighs again. "I'm used to it Cass, it's part of the job. Things like this happen all the time, but I really do have the best fans. Most people respect my space and won't engage in this manhunt. But some will. I'm not worried though. No one will find me here while we are snowed in. And then I'll be camping out at my parents' house for a few days either side of Christmas."

A thought pops into my head. "But don't people know where you grew up? In the early stages of your career, you did that interview with that magazine Rock Gods, and they asked about your hometown. Won't they work out you might have gone home?"

I can hear the panic in my voice, worry consuming me. I take in a few deep breaths, trying to calm myself. It's okay, no one knows he is here right now, and we might stay snowed in anyway.

He angles his head towards me, the corner of his mouth curving up into a smile. "You remember that interview?"

A hot flush, that I know instantly translates to a red blush, crosses my face and chest and I nod quickly before ducking my head.

His hand cups my chin and he lifts it up, my eyes meeting his, before he quickly drops his hand. "Hey, that's a good thing. Do you remember what I said in that interview? About you?"

I nod, "Yeah, how could I forget?"

He told the interviewer who asked about a current relationship back then, that his heart belonged to his first love and always would. It was only a year after we had broken up and I just about left my blossoming career to take off across the country to him. But then a week later, the team I was in was given a project to work on, an innovative wearable medical device, and I was given an associate position as a newly qualified Biomedical Engineer.

I couldn't just up and leave. But my heart desperately wanted to.

Our lives are worlds apart, his so completely different from my own and it's hard to believe that we started in the same place.

But despite the huge differences between us, and his mammoth success, he still talks and sounds like the Asher I knew.

Before he can ask anything further about that interview, I jump in with another question, hoping to redirect the conversation.

"Do you like it? The fame I mean. Is all of that, the phone call stuff, worth it?"

He seems to consider my question for a moment, running his hand through his hair, the soft strands falling back perfectly into place, and I'm reminded instantly of when he does that on stage. Women and men go wild for it. I do too.

"Yeah, oddly enough, it is worth it. I get that there's some hairy moments like that one earlier, but every day I wake up and do what I love with my best friends, my bandmates. But yeah, some days I do wish I wasn't famous and could live a normal life. All jobs have their downside. It's been everything I wanted… mostly. Sometimes it's… lonely too." We sit in silence for a moment, his last comment hitting a nerve. I get lonely too.

I bump him with my elbow, hoping to lighten the mood.

"I went to one of your concerts," I tell him shyly. "It was freakishly good Asher. You've done well. Better than well. Proud of you."

He turns to stare at me, a genuine smile of surprise crossing his face.

"You came to one of my concerts… that means a lot Peaches. More than you know. You were my biggest supporter all those years ago. You're the reason I even thought I had a chance at this."

I'm floored by his admission, not wanting to take the credit for not having done the work.

"No Asher, that was all you. I just believed in you is all."

"You're wrong Cassidy. It was so much more than that."

I refuse to believe it, shaking my head and focusing on smoothing my dress over my knees.

He's wrong. There's no way I had that much influence over him making it big. He sells out stadiums worldwide. He has fifty million followers on his social media account.

No way did I have any hand in helping him on his way.

He bumps his knee into mine.

"So, you came to one of my concerts. Which one was it?"

I laugh softly, smiling over at him, embarrassed to admit I was fangirling in his crowd.

But I was fangirling. Hard.

"It was your concert at Magnitude Stadium. It was surreal… you were amazing Asher."

He looks up at the ceiling humming for a moment before snapping his fingers, pointing at me.

"Summer of 2016, right?"

Surprise flashes through me. "You can so easily remember a concert from that long ago?"

He nods, chuckling. "I can remember them all. I've never taken this life I get to live for granted. I'm grateful for all the shows I've gotten to perform. And for all the shows I God willing, get to continue to do."

His eyes find mine, his stare burning hot and I feel a tingle creeping up my arms. I shiver, and he reaches over to pull my cardigan over my arms.

It's not the temperature in the room making me shiver.

I face forward, glancing down the stairs towards the loud dining room. Laughter rings out and the smell of dinner wafts up the stairs.

I know we should head down, but neither of us make a move to go anywhere.

We sit in a comfortable silence, and I think back over his words.

He really does love what he is doing. For the first time, maybe ever, a little of that heartache I tucked away all those years ago when we broke up, falls away, knowing it might have been the hardest moment of my life, but it led him to a life that he loves.

Chapter 5

As we make our way downstairs, the soft tune of Jingle Bells rings out, and I notice for the first time, the red and white peppermint candy canes in a big, beautiful glass jar, placed on the shelves by the front door. A large red bow adorns the banister, and twinkly lights wind their way up the stairs. Antique gold bells hang from a beautiful green wreath on the wall.

It's beautifully classic.

I wonder if I should book in to stay here every year. Make it a tradition.

We join the other guests in the dining room, where the couples are already seated. They call out their greetings to me and introduce themselves to Asher.

They are all travelling together and are the absolute sweetest. They have been lifelong friends who all met in their early twenties. I marvel at having a friendship that long, over forty years' worth of memories. I don't have a close friendship like that with anyone. When would I have the time with how busy work is. And my coworkers are just that. Colleagues.

Esme and Ted were the first couple I met when I arrived. They were high school sweethearts and still act like the teenagers of the group. Then there's Florence and Bernie who are much more serious but then I've overheard some of the jokes they have cracked, and I don't think I've blushed that much ever. Finally, there's Lorenzo and Alessandra who both greeted me with a warm hug and who instantly put me at ease.

Asher is kind and friendly, greeting them individually, and if I didn't know better, I would not think he was a famous singer in a rock band.

He's down to earth and good natured, warm and friendly. I feel oddly relieved. Although my gut tells me he is still the same Asher, I haven't seen him in years so I can't know for sure.

I had thought that fame would have changed him, but that spark we always had, still feels like it burns just as strong.

Charisma oozes from him. He has that 'rockstar swagger' and his presence demands attention. He makes small talk, charming the other guests as we pass their tables, the small group eating up everything he says.

As we pass Sawyer's table, I give him a quick but fleeting smile, butterflies dancing in my stomach. He glares at us as we pass, and we come to a stop at the empty table in the corner.

Pearl is busily placing more dinnerware out, so we stand and wait. "Sorry dears, this won't take a minute."

Asher steps close and leans down to whisper in my ear. A zap shoots through me, when I feel his warm breath at my neck.

"What's his problem?" I turn my face to his, our noses almost touching. I run my tongue over my lips, and his eyes track my movement. I see his pronounced swallow and when I speak my words are breathy, against my better judgment.

"Don't worry, it's not you. I think it's everyone. He doesn't seem to like anyone here. And the snowstorm too. He hasn't been happy since he got here. Just ignore him."

He scowls, glancing over his shoulder again. He looks a little apprehensive when he turns to face me.

"Do you think he would tell anyone I'm here?"

I shrug my shoulders, a little doubt creeping in. "I don't know. I don't think so. Pearl made it clear to everyone that they are not to tell a single soul that you're here."

I know I don't sound reassuring at all, and I want to be, but I just don't know about this guy.

Pearl steps back, beaming at us. "How serendipitous that you are both here after not seeing each other for so long! This is just wonderful."

She gives us a little wave and disappears, leaving us to take our seats. I can now see what took her so long. She has set up candles and placed a single rose in a vase on our table.

She's such a sweet lady.

I glance around at the other tables, which are very noticeably devoid of those two things. I quickly take a seat at the table and Asher slides into his.

"So, you told Pearl about us?" He holds his hands up in the air, feigning innocence but that mischievous smile is back.

"Who me?" He says with a playful grin.

I can't help but laugh at his expression. Butter wouldn't melt, honestly, and it's always been that way.

"Yes, you."

"Yeah, I did… I'm sorry. She cornered me when I came down for afternoon tea, and she wanted to know how we knew each other. She was very excited, it was nice."

I don't mind, I'm just giving him a hard time. Pearl and Dusty seem like sweet souls and I'm certain they mean well and wouldn't out us in any way.

My identity has largely remained a secret, and I would like to keep it that way. I remember his fans commenting all over social media, trying to find out who Asher Mills' first love was. I have a sneaking suspicion that his team squashed that because every time they came close, comments were removed and something else was released from Ash & Stone to distract the public.

Our meals are served, a large roast dinner with all the fixings. The fireplace is crackling in the background and the festive melody of Christmas tunes, play softly from the speakers.

"Some red wine for your date?" Pearl says, giving us a mischievous smile. She pours us both a glass of red wine and as we eat, we share laughs and funny stories of his time on tour and my work team.

It feels normal, like we are two people out on a date, getting to know each other. Or in our case, reacquainted.

When Pearl brings over the wine again, neither of us say no.

Eventually she leaves the bottle with a wink and before long the dining room is empty, and it's just us and the roaring fireplace.

I yawn, realising just how tired I am. The wine has made my bones feel soft and warm, and if there was someplace to close my eyes and sleep right now, I would.

I stand from the table and stretch, a warm flush covering my body.

I'm definitely tipsy.

Asher stands slowly, his eyes tracing a path from my waist up, before they land on my own.

It's then that I notice his wallet has fallen to the ground. I crouch down to pick it up and it falls open, face up.

My mouth drops and I bring the wallet closer to my face. I must have had more to drink than I thought.

I take another look. It's exactly as I see it.

A picture of us, folded over and tucked into his wallet, from when we were dating. Our young and in love faces stare up at me and I pull the picture out the rest of the way, mesmerised by it. It's one of those three in one photo booth shots.

I remember that date so well.

We were nineteen and had just moved in together. We were still in that 'it's fun to grocery shop' phase and were grabbing some items when we spotted a photo both on our way out.

We jumped in and took a photo, holding up our receipt, laughing together. I unravel it. The next photo is us kissing and the third photo has me taking in a shaky breath.

I'm smiling wide at the camera and Asher is looking at me. His expression is tender and very clearly, in love.

My eyes shoot up to his. He doesn't look embarrassed. He looks relieved.

He takes my hand, helping me up and I hand his wallet and the picture back to him.

"I can't believe you still have that old picture. Why do you have that in your wallet Asher?" I ask him slowly.

He raises his eyebrows, looking me directly in the eye, unashamedly. "You know why Peaches."

That's it. That's all he says.

I shake my head in confusion. "No, I don't."

He takes a step closer to me after tucking the photo back into his wallet carefully and then into his pocket.

"Come here and I'll show you." Before I can say another word, he steps closer and wraps his arms around my waist, drawing me flush with his chest.

"Oh," is all I can muster.

My heart is racing and warmth pools between my legs when I feel his hard length press against me.

"Tell me to stop and I'll step away, I promise Peaches. The ball's in your court. It always has been."

I should tell him to stop but I don't want to.

"Don't stop."

He groans and crashes against my mouth, our tongues moving together, both desperate for entry. He softly bites my lip, and I moan, my hands reaching up to tangle in his hair, while his hands move up and down my body like he wants to touch me everywhere. He slides his hand down my thigh to my knee, hiking it up and wrapping it around his hip. He grinds against me, and my ankle digs into his thigh, needing to be closer.

He peppers kisses down my neck, trailing a path down my chest. He pulls my bra away from my skin and his tongue darts under the lace, lapping at my nipple, sucking it into his mouth. Electricity shoots down to my core and I slip my hands underneath his t-shirt, running them over his stomach and around to his back. His skin is soft and warm, taut with muscles. I dip my hands into the back of his briefs, and he thrusts against me.

His mouth finds mine again, and his hand cups my shoulder, slipping his fingers underneath the strap there to lower the top half of my dress. I whisper "More," to him and his heavy breathing gets even louder.

Suddenly, I hear voices at the door before Pearl steps into the room. "Hello, just checking if you're both finished with din… oh! Oh, I'm so sorry. I'll leave now, carry on," and she hastily leaves the room. Asher turned so quickly I didn't even realise what was happening, covering me from being seen with the top of my dress hanging down.

It feels as though someone has thrown a bucket of water on me, and I drop my leg and slide my hands out from under his shirt, taking a shaky step back.

I smooth down my dress and lift the strap back up. "Uh, dinner was lovely Asher. I didn't realise the time; I better be headed to bed. Good night," I mutter awkwardly.

I grab my purse and slip out of the room as fast as I can. I stop at the bottom of the stairs and cover my face with my hands. What am I doing, making out with my seriously gorgeous, mega famous ex-boyfriend?

Correction. Not only my ex, but also the only man I've ever loved.

A glimmer of hope sparks in my chest. He still has our picture in his wallet. That counts for a hell of a lot of somethings.

Chapter 6

I TOSS AND TURN ALL night.

That damn kiss has me twisted up inside.

It doesn't help that after I went to bed, I heard Asher next door, softly strumming his guitar, singing some crooning melody, that had me melting all over again.

It was so different to his usual rock songs. The melody is soothing and if my brain wasn't racing, I could easily fall asleep to his voice.

Except I can't.

Because all I can think about are his hands and mouth roaming my body downstairs in the dining room. Flash backs to our relationship also make an appearance.

It was a passionate one. We were together for six years and that fire between us, didn't once flicker out. Even after we said our goodbyes.

I remember the day it all went down, because I've replayed it in my brain so many times.

Well, really it was months in the making, not just one particular day. When I first met Asher, he was seventeen turning eighteen, and I was sixteen, not far off seventeen. He was lead guitarist and singer with his friends in their band, Ash & Stone. His two school friends and brothers, made up the rest of the band. Foster Stone was and still is, the drummer and Kit Stone the bassist. They had been playing together for years and were phenomenal already.

Not to mention, they were just a good group of guys.

The night I met Asher, they were the opening band for another local group that was on its way up, and I went to see their show. It was just like the movies, and I had a hard time believing it myself at the time.

Our eyes met during one of his songs and that was it.

He asked for my number after the show, and we spent every day together after.

For six years, we weren't apart for more than a couple of days.

We were young and in love with our future all mapped out. We were going to graduate school, then university, and after we would travel together when his band made it big. I was going to put my career dreams on hold. Or so I thought at the time. That all changed not long after I started school and fell in love with my chosen career field.

It was a given they would make it big, even if Asher had a hard time believing it. We went to the same university and spent those four years in two different headspaces.

Our love for each other never changed, in fact it only grew stronger, but our career plans certainly did.

Asher's degree in teaching was a fall-back option, if his music career crashed and burned. But he hated it.

I knew his music career wouldn't crash and burn, and I continued to encourage him to keep applying to competitions and for music grants with producers.

One day, their hard work paid off, and they won a six-month mentorship with a big-time music producer, and the rest is history. He saw their potential from day one.

The following day, Asher dropped out of university after three and a half years of study, deciding instead to bet on himself and his band.

It was around this time, that I realised I wouldn't be able to just walk away from my career. I was desperate to get started in that field once my studies were over and on my final placement, the clinical director of the company told me I had a promising future and offered me a job for when I finished. I was ecstatic and believed we could make it work.

Six months into Ashers mentorship and right around the time university finished for me, their song hit the charts reaching number ten and steadily making its way to number one.

I kept putting off the conversation with Asher, hoping a solution would just magically materialise.

It didn't.

One afternoon, we went into the studio, and he was accosted by fans. Hundreds of people lined the studio streets as our car pulled in.

At that stage, I was still flying under the radar, his fans not having caught on that we were together yet. His social media profile was still private back then.

He jumped out of the car and waved to his fans, before reaching in to take my hand. I could feel the panic crawling up my throat and I shook my head, whispering "I'm sorry, I can't."

I remember his expression so well. He looked shattered.

He began to hop back into the car, but I waved him back out, reassuring him I would be fine and that I just wanted to head home.

He stood on that sidewalk, his fans going wild around him, not once taking his eyes off the car as I was driven away.

I cried the whole trip back to our apartment, and it hit me all at once.

I knew I didn't want to be in the light of fame, even as his partner, and I knew I wanted to be a Biomedical Engineer.

My dream job wasn't travelling and being a groupie.

But he was my everything. We sat down that evening and had the most heartbreaking conversation of my life. We both cried and held each other for hours, until the sun came up.

He pleaded with me to try long distance, but I couldn't. I wouldn't. I had seen people try and always fail, and I didn't have the heart to see him slowly fade out of my life.

It had to be a clean break. And it was.

We spent the following days packing our belongings. His went into storage so he could travel with the band and mine was sold or taken with me to go stay with my sister while I found a place to live near my new job.

I've regretted every day since. Not the following my dream part. I'll never regret that.

But that I just walked away, terribly heartbroken, never allowing myself to crack and reach out.

And he never reached out to me either. Not directly any way. Over the years he produced two songs with Ash & Stone, that I'm certain were about our relationship.

I lie here now, staring at the ceiling, my frustration growing. My heart is pounding through my chest, and I try to take some deep breaths to calm myself, but it's not working. My legs itch to move and I sit up, kicking off the blankets, placing my bare feet on the slightly cool floorboards.

The rest of the room is toasty from the heating, and it usually feels like my own little warm cave.

But right now, it feels too hot, and my skin is crawling.

I don't bother putting any shoes on and instead, I march to the door and pull it open forcefully.

I take the few small steps to his door and not giving myself time to talk my way out of doing this, I knock.

I hear his bed creak and what sounds like a lamp being turned on.

Heavy footsteps sound and my nerves creep back in, twisting and turning in my stomach.

Before I can run away, his door swings open and my breath catches in my throat.

He's only wearing sweatpants. And they hang low on his angular hips.

My instant thought is that I would love to run my finger along the inside of those pants. I shake my head, trying to rid myself of that thought, knowing I probably look crazy.

I force myself to look up at his face and away from his muscular body that even from a metre away, I can feel is radiating heat, hotter than the internal temperature in the inn.

He yawns, pushing the hair out of his eyes. He is wearing glasses. Well, that's new.

Oh lord, help me.

Why is this man getting hotter as he ages? It's unfair really that he should look so good.

He leans his arm against the door frame, slowly taking me in. His eyes widen when he sees what I'm wearing. I remember then that I'm only wearing an oversized tee.

But not just any tee.

His uni t-shirt that I staked claim of, in his first year. The one that I wear to bed religiously, unless it's in the wash.

I could die right now.

Felix always thought it was mine because I went to the same school. And I did feel bad that I let him believe that.

He clears his throat, "Cassidy… is everything okay?" His voice is raspy, hoarse from sleep.

I don't answer him and instead I jump straight into my question. If I don't, I'll lose my nerve and slither back to my room in a puddle of embarrassment.

"Why didn't you ever reach out? After you left." He looks taken aback by my question. He stands upright, crossing his arms. The nerves in my stomach dive again.

"After I left? Do you mean when I went on tour? Because I didn't leave you Peaches… I never would have. You told me it wouldn't work and to not try to change your mind, because it was made up." His voice is dripping with annoyance.

He's right. I did say that. It was hard, even though I knew it was the right thing to do.

"Cass after you moved out, I picked up that phone every day, multiple times in the day, to call you, but couldn't bring myself to actually dial the number. It was the hardest thing I've ever had to go through. I hated it. But I hated the thought of forcing you on tour or making you do long distance when you were very clear, that was not an option. You're too brilliant to just tag along with me. I've followed your career over the years Cass and you're amazing. I can't even fathom how you do what you do. The medical equipment you have helped create for hospitals. And your presentation to that big symposium you did. I watched it online. You blow me away."

I blush at his words, but the earlier ones fall on me the hardest. I wonder what would have happened if he had of pressed call, each time he picked up the phone.

Asher reaches out, lightly tugging on my shirt, his fingers trailing along my leg. My leg tingles, feeling the loss when his fingers leave my skin. "This is nice… and unexpected. It looks better on you than it ever did on me Peaches."

I flash him a small smile, taking a step back. Emotion weighs heavy on my chest, my eyes beginning to well. I don't want him to see me cry right now.

"It's late… I'm sorry I interrupted you. Night Asher."

He leans against the door frame, resting his head there.

"Night, Cassidy Blake," he says softly.

I move back to my room, closing the door behind me. I crawl onto the bed, up towards the headboard, pulling the thick, fluffy quilt up to my neck, sinking back into the pillows. The tears flow thick and fast, unchecked down my face.

Chapter 7

I WAKE UP THE NEXT morning with a crying jag hangover.

I cried on and off, albeit quietly so that Asher couldn't hear me through the wall, for the rest of the night before falling into an exhausted sleep.

All these thoughts ran through my head. Did I make the right decision after all? Should I have chosen him and not the career? Why, didn't we fight for it?

My head is aching, and my eyes are burning.

I pick up the phone and call Pearl at the reception desk.

"I'm not feeling so great this morning Pearl… is it possible to please get breakfast sent up to my room? Oh, thank you. You're wonderful."

I hang up and lay back down, curling into a ball before closing my eyes. Not even twenty minutes later, there's a solid knock on my door. Pearl had said she would leave it at the door for me, so I don't rush to get up. I don't want her seeing my face right now anyway.

I can just imagine what would greet her. A splotchy, puffy, red face with mascara streaks down my cheeks and chin. My hair must also be a sight as I left it out overnight. A bird's nest would aptly describe it, I'm sure.

I blow my nose and wipe away a fresh wave of tears.

A knock at the door sounds again, this time even louder. Maybe the food is a trip hazard at the door, and she has decided not to leave it. I guess the hallway is quite small.

"Argh."

I swing my legs over the side of the bed, before shuffling to the door, still in my tee from last night. I plaster a smile on my face, hoping it will distract her from the sight she is about to see.

I open the door just a fraction, ducking my head to the side. "Thanks so much Pe…" My voice trails off, caught in my throat when I see that it isn't Pearl at the door. It's Asher.

Holding my breakfast tray with a concerned look on his face.

"What's happened?" He asks, his voice hardening when he sees my tear streaked, red face. I remember how fiercely protective Asher was, and I guess probably still is.

A fresh wave of tears forms, pooling in my eyes before falling in fast, hot drips, down my face. His expression becomes pained, and he pushes the door open further, stepping past me to put the tray down on the table before turning and reaching out for me, pulling me flush against his chest. Dammit he smells good.

"I could never stand to see you cry and that hasn't changed. Please tell me what's happened Peaches. Do I need to have a word with someone?"

That makes me cry even harder. He is such a wonderful man, and I just threw it all away.

He rubs soothing circles into my back with one hand, the other softly stroking my hair. He leans back for a moment, the hand that was stroking my hair, moving to cup my cheek before sliding down and tilting my chin up.

"Talk to me. I know it's been a long time… but it's me." He looks so earnest and open that I blurt it all out before I can stop myself.

"We walked away from each other," I say, my words breaking. "And I know it needed to happen for us to follow our passions, but we didn't even try another way. I've missed you all this time. And don't get me wrong, I love my job, but was it worth losing you? I don't know. Maybe? No, it definitely wasn't. I wish we could just go back in time."

I'm spiralling, my words a jumbled mess, my thoughts spewing from my mouth as they pop into my head. He rubs my cheek with his thumb, searching my eyes, a brief flash of torment betraying his emotions.

"Hey. You're right, we didn't fight hard enough. But I remember that determined glint in your eye. That passion and excitement you had for your career. I had that too. If we had stayed together, one of us would have sacrificed everything for the other. We were too young to make it work long distance or try any other way. We were so consumed by each other that we would have left one of our jobs to be with the other and then grown to resent each other for it. It would have ended with us breaking up, hating each other."

He's making a lot of sense. It's the same thing I've told myself for years but faced with him now and all these resurfacing feelings, it's hard to be rational.

A hiccup escapes me, and I draw in a deep breath holding it, trying to rid them.

It doesn't work and my next hiccup is even louder. Asher's smile turns gentle, soft and he continues. "But look at us now Cass. Here we are again, getting along more than fine, no anger or resentment between us. Yes, some regret, but I would be worried if we didn't have that at all."

I sniff, brushing the tears from underneath my eyes.

"When did you get so wise huh?" I mumble, unable to stop myself from giving him a small smile when he laughs.

"I wouldn't go that far. But I have grown up, I can promise you that." He lifts my hand and turns it over, tracing the lines there. His fingers are rough, calloused in places from years of playing guitar, yet softer in other spots. "Remember when we went to that fair and saw the psychic? She looked at both of our palms and said, and I quote 'Your lifelines are the same. Your lives will be forever entwined'".

My laugh is watery, remembering how excited we were by what she had told us. It solidified to us that we were meant to be together. Another thought creeps in, confirming my suspicions.

"Forever entwined… your song. You did write that about us." He nods but doesn't say anything. I scramble to think of the lyrics, softly humming the tune before I quietly sing a few of the words. "Distance can't tame us, or quieten our love song. No matter where you go, I'll be with you, always there to support, always right behind you. I'll be cheering you on from afar, until we meet again, you're my quiet light in the dark, you're my best friend. You're my everything."

After the first line, he joins me, and we sing it together. I forgot how much we both enjoyed singing together. He would practice his songs, and I would sing back up and occasionally provide a drum solo on the laundry bucket. It was magic.

He continues tracing the lines on my hand before he reaches down to kiss my palm. His bottom lip is soft and a little fuller than the top, and the stubble on his chin tickles my palm.

"Come on, your breakfast is getting cold." He keeps my hand firmly in his, leading me over to the cosy wingback chair, overlooking the small frozen lake outside. I take a seat, and he brings the tray over, placing it on the small table next to me.

He leans down, kissing my cheek and my pulse jumps, goosebumps breaking out over my skin.

"I'm going to leave you to eat breakfast Peaches. Would you like to go for a walk with me this morning?" I nod eagerly, keen for fresh air and more time with him.

I want to savour this as much as I can, knowing that each day brings us closer to the roads being open, and us parting ways.

Chapter 8

I sat by the window enjoying my breakfast of scrambled eggs, bacon, fruit and hot coffee for longer than I expected I would. I watched the snow fall, coating the trees and the soft grass, before slowing to stop and then starting back up again. The wind is a lot gentler today, swirling snow across the frozen lake and I wonder if the roads will be open again soon.

Lost in thought, I watch the rhythmic dance between the sky and the earth, and where the snow chooses to land. It's beautiful and grounding. The floor heating filters through vents right where I'm sitting, so my feet stay warm.

I admire the room from this spot, really taking it all in for the first time. Pearl and Dusty have strung a Christmas garland around the window frame and across the dresser top, and red tartan pillows adorn the bed and this chair, along with a cosy forest green blanket.

The rest of the room is crisp white with brown wooden accents, from the furniture and exposed beams, to the antique floorboards, dresser and beside tables.

After I finish breakfast, I have some time to review my notes for a project I'm working on that's going to be innovative in the health care system. I send off a few quick emails to my team, asking for updates on their progress.

All in all, the morning was a much better one than expected, given the night before.

I sink back into the chair once the final email is sent and glance over at the clock. I got so lost in what I was doing and enjoying the view from my window, that I didn't realise it is nearing lunchtime. I promised Asher I would take a walk around the grounds and I refuse to go out looking like this again. Excitement builds in my belly at the thought of seeing him.

I leave my cosy chair in favour of a hot shower. I wash my hair and a night of crying away. My hair is matted in strands from being soaked with tears all night.

I feel better already as I towel dry myself, with the softest cotton fabric, in the most gorgeous pine green colour. I throw on a pair of jeans, a large, oversized sweater, thick socks and snow boots.

I blow-dry my hair and put a little mascara on. My usual routine. I don't usually bother with anything more than that.

As I race down the stairs, I almost trip on the last step, colliding with Asher. He steadies me, grabbing hold of both of my forearms.

"Woah, I've got you." I give him a quick smile.

"I was hoping to 'run' into you, but not like this." He gives me a warm smile in return.

"Are you ready for that walk?" I nod eagerly, not caring to hide my excitement.

We've never been anything but transparent and totally upfront with each other and I'm certainly not stopping that now.

He pulls a thick pair of gloves from his pocket, frowning when he looks down at my hands. "Where are your gloves? And your scarf, your beanie?"

I smile sheepishly. "I kind of left home in a rush. This trip wasn't exactly planned and so I didn't give myself a lot of time to get snow gear. It's been a while since I've done a snowy Christmas."

He tilts his head to the side, a loose tendril of hair falling into his eyes. Without a second thought, I reach up and gently push it out of the way, my cheeks flushing pink.

He catches my hand softly as I lower it.

"Let's come back to that. But wait here a moment." He runs up the stairs, disappearing down the corridor when he reaches the top step.

I wander over to the Christmas tree and run my fingers along the branches and the spiky needles. Just like the rest of the inn, it's tastefully decorated with gold and silver glass baubles, and a matching star on top.

We always had a real Christmas tree growing up, but the last few years I haven't had time to get one, let alone a real one. I decide then, that next year I will get a real tree, just like this one.

He doesn't keep me waiting long, returning with a bundle in his arms. When he reaches the bottom step, I start to move towards the front door, before he stops me.

"You're not going out in that cold dressed like that Cass. You'll freeze. Let me fix that for you." He holds out a scarf, draping it around my neck, before not only giving me gloves, but also putting them on for me. They are soft and warm.

Finally, he pulls a beanie from his pocket and places it on my head. His hands slide down, squeezing my shoulders before moving down to my wrists.

"There, that should keep you warm." He clears his throat, his voice hoarse. "Let's go Peaches." He holds his hand out and I can't explain it, but it feels symbolic to me, to take his hand.

Like this is more than just a walk around the grounds of the inn we are snowed in at.

I take his hand, realising then, that he doesn't have any gloves on.

"Oh, I didn't realise I took your only pair." I pull my hand from his, trying to extricate it from the glove, but his hand gently takes mine again.

"I don't care. You know that."

I do know that. I always came first. Nothing was ever too hard, too much of a hassle. He was the epitome of a supportive and nurturing partner.

But it wasn't meant to be back then. Now, we both have our thriving careers, and fate has brought us back together. Could now be the right time?

We step out onto the verandah, waving to Florence and Bernie, who are sitting out on the wicker chairs with a coffee, the steam swirling in the air.

Pearl steps out from behind us with a plate of pastries and Christmas cookies. They smell like butter, cinnamon and sugar, and my mouth waters.

Holding the plate out towards us, she winks. "A cookie for your walk honeys?"

I eagerly grab one, taking a bite instantly. It's soft and gooey, still warm from the oven. Asher grabs a cookie too, taking a big bite.

"Wow, Pearl these are incredible," he says, mouth full. He grins, adding, "I think this is the best cookie I've ever had."

Pearl blushes, fanning her face. She is so endearing.

"You flatter me honey, thank you. Be careful out there, the forecast says another snowstorm could breeze in later. At this stage, the roads are still too thick with ice, so everything remains closed unfortunately."

She pats my arm sympathetically, before moving on to the other guests to offer them a baked treat. I don't tell her that I don't mind that we are snowed in for a few more days.

I step down onto the stairs and Asher grabs my hand again. I can feel the warmth of his hand through my soft gloves, and we make our way down the stairs, turning left once we hit the path. Dusty must have been out here this morning ploughing a track around the inn, because a small path opens up before us. It's narrow, forcing us closer together.

He drops my hand, and I feel the loss of his warmth instantly. But instead of holding my hand, he wraps his arm around my shoulder, dropping a kiss to the top of my head. I had forgotten how well I fit just under his arm and how safe it feels. It feels like home and it's a sobering thought.

"So, let's talk about why you didn't have time to pack before coming here. What's going on Cass?"

I place the rest of my cookie in my pocket, my appetite suddenly gone.

"I was in a relationship before I came here. It was over a long time ago though. I should have left him earlier than I did. But we were dating for so long… three years all up. The first year was easy. Nice. We worked in the same department, and we still work together but different areas now. He understood my work and was interested in my day, in what I did. But as time went on, I realised he was interested in only my work, and not so much me. I took a backseat to his job and his friends, and honestly, I just got so tired of it."

Without even noticing, we stopped walking. Asher looks furious. He rests his hands behind his head, his eyes narrowing the more I talk. His chest rises and falls fast, as he takes in a few deep breaths.

Do I keep going? I decide to tell him the rest, despite his clear anger.

"So um, he's also been rejected for promotions at work, while I've been steadily moving up the ladder. I understand how hard that would be, but it built resentment in him that worsened as time went on. We weren't living together, so it wasn't like I had to pack and run. I just hadn't planned on coming home for Christmas this year, so my decision was last minute. He hated Christmas and so I haven't been home in a few years. Or anywhere this cold actually. Hence why I don't have gloves or a scarf," I ramble, laughing awkwardly.

If it's even possible, he looks more pissed than he did a few minutes ago.

"He sounds like a piece of shit Peaches. And it's making me angry the more I hear about him. I hate hearing about you being with someone else but knowing he stopped you from going home for Christmas? When it's something you love so much. Yeah, I'm fucking angry. If we ever come across him, be sure to point him out to me so I can have a nice little conversation with him."

I move to touch his face, before I drop my hand, pulling off my glove. I reach up again and cradle his cheek, wanting to feel him. The stubble on his cheek prickles my fingers, and there's a dark shadow highlighting his jaw.

I've always loved when he has some growth. It makes him look wild and rugged and my mind flashes back to that men's underwear advertisement he did a few years ago.

It's freezing out here, but suddenly I feel hot, a little sweaty even.

The advert was a television commercial of Asher, in black briefs, posing with his guitar. A few other shots included him standing naked, strategically holding his guitar.

I had to stop checking the comments on social media because I was in a constant state of embarrassment at the things people said about him. I didn't know people could be so honestly depraved, especially in such a public forum.

If I had thought Asher was fit all those years ago, that's nothing compared to him right now. Asher at forty-one, is in better shape than most men in their twenties and thirties. His arms are strong and muscled, veins corded through his forearms, and his legs are the same. When he came to the door last night in just sweats, I saw every inch of his powerful abs and chest.

And Asher talking about having words with Felix? Hot.

I love his protective side and I'm not ashamed to admit it. Asher was always good at being there for me if I needed his help, but also believing in my ability to handle things. I never believed I was very strong, but with Asher, I reached a stage of feeling at least a little invincible.

Hearing his words now, especially after dating Felix for so long, who didn't care about anything, makes me feel all the things.

"I'll be sure to point him out. But he honestly isn't worth my time. Or yours. I'm up for another promotion at work soon and if I get it, I'll be changing departments, which means a new building too. I probably won't ever see him."

He hums his agreement. "You'll get it Peaches. And I still want you to point him out. Anyone else we need to add to the list?"

I stare up at him in confusion. "What list?"

His smile is indulgent, and I melt a little under it.

"The list I'm compiling of everyone who has done you wrong in the last seventeen years. The names of the people I need to have a shit ton of words with."

My heart thumps uncomfortably fast in my chest and butterflies dance in my stomach. I swallow loudly, my throat suddenly so dry.

"Thank you for that. It means… everything to me."

He shakes his head, putting his arm around me and we continue walking "I'm just sorry I wasn't there for any of it Peaches. The highs, the lows, the shitty people like your ex. I actually hate hearing you even had an ex."

I totally get it. I don't want to hear about any of his ex-partners, and I don't think I'm brave enough to even ask, so I won't.

We walk in a comfortable silence for a few minutes, making our way into the back garden. The snow isn't as thick here and we veer off the path, making our way to the gazebo. Snow covers the roof and the twinkly lights inside, make it look even more inviting.

There's an outdoor fireplace and it's roaring. Pearl has left flasks of hot coffee and mugs out on the table, more pastries and a little note that reads; *Hopefully this will warm you up after your walk xo'*. She thinks of everything.

We step under the awning and take a seat at the table, sliding in across from each other. Asher reaches over and grabs one of the thick fluffy blankets, placing it across my lap and I tuck my feet up under me and settle in against the cushion behind me.

He watches me amused and a blush colours my cheeks again. When will I ever stop blushing around this man?

The heat from the fireplace warms my cheeks even more and I let out a content sigh.

Christmas wreathes adorn the wooden gazebo poles and it makes the space feel even more homely. Snow has started to fall in soft sprinkles, dusting the benches and the trees, reminding me of icing sugar.

It's magical.

Asher pours us piping hot coffee and my hands circle the mug, the heat warming them.

We talk about his life on tour, about his family and how they are doing. How his sister and brother both have children and how much he adores and spoils them when he gets to see them. He shows me sweet pictures of his family joining him briefly on tour and we laugh at his nieces and nephews on stage pretending to sing before the concert started.

I tell him a little more about my career and some of the devices I have designed that have helped save lives. I'm proud of the work I've done and happy to share it.

"I was blown away when I watched you present at that con-ference. I didn't understand most of what you said, but it was hypnotic watching you speak. You were made for this Cass. And it was sexy as hell." He moves to crouch down by the fireplace, stoking the fire and adding some more wood.

I drift into a dream state for a moment, where I can almost imagine this being our little home, on a lazy Sunday afternoon.

I reach for a pastry on auto pilot, taking a bite, replaying what our life would look like over and over, completely lost in the fantasy. Would we have kids? Where would we live? Would we do a big family Christmas'?

"Peaches, are you okay? Where'd you go just then?"

"Oh, I was daydreaming. About us," I let slip.

Oh no, shit. I didn't mean to blurt that out. My face flushes with embarrassment.

Asher's eyebrows shoot up in surprise and his breath catches. "I do that all the time Peaches."

Now it's my turn to be surprised. "You daydream too?"

"Yeah. I daydream about us. All the freakin' time."

Chapter 9

"You wwhat?" I stutter.

His mouth curls up on one side in a smile I know all too well, and goosebumps pop up along my skin.

He repeats himself, adding, "Peaches, you were the absolute love of my life. Do you think I would just forget about you and move on? No one has come close to you all this time and no one ever will."

His words hang in the air, his expression serious. He means it. And I'm at a loss for words.

Thankfully, I'm saved by Pearl stepping up into the gazebo. I hadn't even heard her approaching.

"Hello darlings, lunch is ready! Dusty has made a warm pumpkin soup with thick, buttered bread."

Right on cue, my stomach grumbles. I push the chair back and say brightly, on the verge of some kind of a meltdown, "Wonderful sounds lovely Pearl. Let's go!"

I give Asher a quick smile, that probably borders on crazy. But he knows me too well. He turns his head to the side, narrowing his eyes slightly.

And I know him just as well. He's totally onto me. The panic slowly rises up from my stomach, consuming me. I race down the stairs, marching ahead of them and quickly excuse myself when we get inside, thundering upstairs to my bedroom.

I pace the floor, door to wall, and then suddenly change direction heading towards the window. I unlock the latch and slide the window up, sticking my head out, taking in deep, lung filling breaths.

I close my eyes, head hanging out the window, knowing if someone walked past right now, they would think I was crazy.

And I probably am, but I just don't have it in me to care right now.

I don't know what to do with what he just said in the garden. But what I'm fast discovering is that we seem to be on the same wavelength.

I never imagined in all these years, he would feel the same as I do. His little admissions the past two days, coupled with the photos in his wallet have me feeling overwhelmed.

I've just gotten out of a relationship, and I told myself I would stay single for a while. It's not even been a few weeks.

Besides, he's a big time rockstar and I'm well… me.

I'm good at what I do, great actually, and I'm also a good person. But 'rockstar still having feelings for me seventeen years later', kind of great? Unlikely.

Doubt begins to eat at me as I withdraw my head from out of the window. A storm is rolling in and foreboding clouds blanket the sky, hiding the sun from view. It feels like it's already evening.

I flick the bedside lamp on, the room bathed in darkness except for that light. It makes the space more intimate and inviting somehow, but I'm too focussed on my thoughts to enjoy it.

I begin to pace the room again. My sensible, logical brain has always disappeared in a puff of smoke, when it comes to Asher.

That's it. I reach for my notepad and pen, sitting on the edge of the bed.

If I use some evidence-based practice here, I could work this out.

I jot a few notes down, gnawing on my pen lid. I need my laptop to research this a little more. Starting with better emotional regulation skills. Then I can make a more informed decision or assess his level of seriousness about us.

I jump up and move to grab my laptop, when a knock on the door interrupts my thought spiral. Do I hold my breath and pretend I'm not here? Maybe whoever it is, will think I'm in the bathroom and leave.

I hear a very distinct Asher sounding sigh on the other side of the door.

"Cassidy, I know you're not in the bathroom and I know you can hear me. You're spiralling, aren't you?"

Damn. I wish he didn't know me so well.

Well, no that's not true at all.

I stride to the door and fling it open, deciding to go with complete honesty, not wanting to keep anything from him this time round.

"Yes, I am. Completely. What you said downstairs… it's shaken me. I thought all this time it was just me that still wanted you. Still had feelings for you. But the things you're saying make it seem like it's not just me. It's you too. Tell me that it's you too."

His chest is heaving at my words, his eyes searching mine. His words tumble from him in a rush.

"Cassidy, I've never stopped loving you and I won't stop. I've missed you, more than you could ever possibly understand." He steps through the door, slamming it shut behind him before taking another step towards me, crushing me to his chest.

Our mouths collide, his tongue pushing for entry into my mouth, at the same time as his hand grabs at my lower back, pulling me even closer to him. I can feel him everywhere and I ache for more.

My hands meet at the back of his neck, my fingers curling into his hair, lightly pulling at the strands.

He groans into my mouth, the sound so raw I can feel it reverberate through my body.

"Can I have you?" He asks, his voice deep and gravelly, going straight to my core.

I don't need any assessment tool to help me work this one out. I want him just as much as he wants me.

"Yes. Please Asher," my voice begs.

He lifts my sweater over my head and tosses it to the floor. I shimmy out of my pants and kick them off as he rips his shirt over his head and pushes his jeans down his legs, both of our actions frenzied, and desperate.

He's not wearing any underwear.

He springs loose when his jeans drop. I reach around and unclip my bra, letting it fall to the floor. His eyes widen and his voice is hoarse.

"Even better than my dreams Peaches. I remember you. I remember this," and he gestures between us. "How could you ever think I would forget us, when this is fucking everything?"

He takes another step towards me, kissing me softly this time. He kisses a path over my cheek and then down from my ear, nipping my shoulder as he passes, before moving down to my chest.

He licks a path across my breasts, stopping to breathe hot air on my nipples, and they harden even more, before he softly closes his mouth over one of the peaks. Asher was always a passionate lover but also a tender one too. The most all-consuming mix of soft and hard.

I run my fingertips down his strong, muscled arms, reaching for his waist, a soft cry tumbling from my lips as his mouth moves to suck on my other nipple. I arch back and his hand shoots around my waist to draw me closer.

Without warning he drops to his knees, grabbing his hard length as he kisses a path down my belly. I grab hold of his shoulders, knowing what's coming next is going to wreck me.

It was always his favourite thing to do, and my god does he do it well. He lightly kisses my underwear, right where I need him and I'm already panting, desperate for more. He runs his tongue down my seam and even through my underwear, I can feel it.

"Mmm, I love when you're ready for me. I can't wait to taste you again. I've definitely dreamed about this too."

His finger hooks into the lace edge of my underwear and pulls it to the side, exposing me to the cool air. He takes in a deep shuddering breath, his hand pumping his hard length fast.

I love watching him pleasure himself and knowing it's me that's turning him on, drives me wild. Suddenly his tongue is there circling me, before he kisses me, sucking hard.

He continues this rhythm and my legs begin to shake, close to buckling under my weight.

"Asher, please don't stop… my god." He pulls back for one moment, grinning up at me, his lips glistening from my arousal.

"Cass, you know how much I love it when you beg."

I groan at his sudden stop, but I can't help the laugh that explodes from me. I shake my head, grabbing the back of his head and gently guiding him back to where he was a moment ago.

His puff of laughter hits me right there, but he doesn't make me wait, his mouth crashing down on me again. His tongue plunges inside of me and curls under, and I can't hold my body upright any longer, overwhelmed by how good this feels. My skin tingles, as if every part of me has been electrified.

I want to cry and beg him for more all at once. I curl over, resting my head on top of his, whimpering. The sensations are almost too much for me to handle, coupled with my own crushing emotions. He stops for a moment, grabbing my face and kissing my mouth.

"I know Peaches, I know."

He rips my underwear down to my ankles and his head moves between my legs again, and this time when his mouth sucks, he dips two fingers inside of me, thrusting in and out. A wave unleashes in my body and soars through me, and I cry out, shaking. I ride the wave up and down, clutching at him to stay upright, but barely holding on.

He removes his fingers from inside of me, kissing me there softly, before planting a kiss to the inside of my thigh and all the way down my leg to my ankle.

I crumble into his arms, and he holds me tightly, softly kissing my cheek.

"Can you handle more Peaches? It's been a long time coming, and I'm not done with you yet."

As if my body is running on an electrical switch, it hums to life again.

"Yes," I answer immediately, suddenly desperate for more. He doesn't waste a second, effortlessly lifting me up and placing me on the bed in one fell swoop. He strips my underwear from my ankles and rests on his forearms, over my body, his head placed just above my hips. He plants another soft kiss down there where I'm tender, but also where I'm suddenly soaking wet again.

He crawls up, unhurried, dragging his hard length up my body, lighting me up everywhere he touches.

I'm squirming and breathless again by the time he reaches me, lining up with my entrance. I reach out, lightly running my fingers up his length, before running back down, stroking him over and over.

I love hearing him come undone and he doesn't disappoint. Groaning in my ear, he growls, "Fuck Cass, if you keep doing that, I'll be done, and I don't want this to be over yet."

He nips at my ear, and I shiver, turning my lips to his. He crushes his mouth to mine and I feel him right where I need him, teasing me. I wrap my legs around his waist, and he pushes in, his throaty groan vibrating into my mouth, when he is all the way inside.

He doesn't move just yet, and we stay like that, pressed together for a few moments. He tenderly kisses my lips, before leaning back a little to look at me. His eyes search mine and the significance of this moment is not lost on me.

This means something to him too.

I never thought we would be back here together. Only in my wildest dreams did I imagine this ever happening again.

He slowly starts to move, and it feels like heaven. The push and stretch is warm and tingly, and each time he is fully in, he hits just the right spot to push me closer to the edge.

His kisses are heated, passionate, and I feel the overwhelming wave of ecstasy beginning in my toes, soaring up through my body.

I fall apart, tucking my head into his neck as I come undone.

A few moments later, Asher explodes, pouring into me and filling me entirely.

We lay there, spent and blissful. Asher pulls me in close and rolls me over so I'm laying across his body. He kisses my mouth, once, twice more, before resting his head back on the pillow. He strokes lazy circles on my arm and over my shoulder and I can feel myself drifting off.

"Peaches… I've missed that. Hell, I've dreamed about that every night for close to two decades."

I hum my agreement. "Me too."

We lay in a comfortable silence for a few minutes, him stroking my arm while I plant soft kisses on his neck.

After a little while, I begrudgingly roll off the bed and make a quick trip to the bathroom to clean up.

We spend the afternoon naked in bed, talking about everything and anything. Our future career goals and plans. But we don't talk about us and what comes next.

Is there even a next? I don't know how, but I really hope so.

We also make up for lost time, kissing and touching constantly. When his hand moves lower over my belly and he dips two fingers inside of me, I get to enjoy another orgasm that rocks me.

That's it. If this doesn't go anywhere beyond this week, I'm remaining celibate for the rest of my life. There is no possible way that I can go back to mediocre sexual partners after this.

"How long are you booked here for?" He interrupts my thoughts, his voice deceptively casual, but he doesn't have me fooled. He must be thinking along the same lines as I am.

"Just till Christmas Eve… I'm planning on surprising my parents then."

My arms tighten a fraction more around him and his do the same. I glance towards the window, watching the snow fall, thicker and more hurried.

It occurs to me then, that I may not even be able to leave Christmas Eve if the snow continues to fall like this.

A pang of disappointment hits me then when I think of the alternative.

Leaving.

I turn back to face Asher and run my hand across his shoulders and down his arm as he pulls the blanket up over my shoulders. The room is bathed in a soft glow from the twinkling fairy lights and the pillows act as a cocoon for us as we lay in bed.

I don't want to leave this bubble.

This perfect moment in time.

Chapter 10

We finally come up for air, deciding we should probably leave our little bubble. Hesitantly though. I could stay here for the rest of the week if I could get Pearl to deliver food for the entirety of my stay.

Actually, that's a thought.

Begrudgingly, I rush Asher out of my room before anyone sees him leaving. He steps into the hallway but spins around quickly, leaning back in through the door, planting a quick kiss to my mouth.

"You're cute Peaches. Don't worry, no one's in the hallway. I'll be respectfully knocking on your door after I shower."

He walks to his door with a chuckle, and I close the door quietly, leaning back against it. That was… something else alright.

If I thought sex with Asher was amazing at twenty-two, then it was out of this world at thirty-nine. Although I didn't want him to leave, I also know I need to be somewhat sensible, and have some space to think.

Like what am I doing exactly? What am I hoping to get out of this… a one-week thing? Something longer?

I need to be realistic too. My phobia of being in the spotlight hasn't changed. Sure, I can get up and present at a conference in front of thousands, but that's a heck of a lot different to people scrutinising me as a person.

And I've seen the partners of rock stars and celebrities get torn to shreds. It's awful.

I need to be careful.

I also can't let this thing between us, whatever it is, affect my work.

I decide then and there that I'm going to talk to him about it tomorrow, when I've had a little more time to think about what I want, and how we could possibly make this work.

Asher knocks on my door, not long after he left, and thankfully amidst my angsty thoughts, I was able to get myself dressed and ready for dinner.

His eyes sparkle when I swing the door open and loudly, he says, "I haven't seen you all day Cass. What have you been up to?"

I roll my eyes at him, but I can't stop the grin that spreads across my face.

"Oh, nothing too interesting. It was a pretty boring day actually…" and before I can finish, he grabs me by the waist and pulls me in close.

He licks the shell of my ear and says softly, "Nothing interesting hey… you weren't saying that when my tongue was inside of you."

I flush as he runs his nose down my neck, softly biting me at my collarbone.

I swallow loudly and clear my throat, but it's still hoarse when I answer.

"Well," I say a little breathless, "That part was pretty good actually…"

He drops his hands from my waist and steps back, crossing his arms, smirking at me.

"Hmmm… I thought so. Let me know when you're up for another 'boring' day." He winks at me and starts walking down the hall.

A laugh bursts from me, and I race to catch up, grabbing his hand quickly and squeezing it, before dropping it again.

I lean up on my tiptoes and whisper in his ear, "I would happily be bored that way, every day of my life. Especially with that tongue of yours…" I drop back down and walk past him this time, hearing his very loud clearing of the throat.

I blush at my own words, and I can't believe I even said that. I mentally hi-five myself.

When I glance back over my shoulder, he is adjusting the front of his pants, and a soft laugh escapes me.

I feel wicked. I'm never like this and it feels fun. I want more.

We make it to the dining room for dinner, and I notice that Sawyer is missing. I haven't actually seen him since yesterday.

"Weird," I mutter.

"What's weird?"

I glance up at Asher confused. Oh, I must have said that out loud.

"Just weird that I haven't seen Sawyer all day. It's a small inn, I just thought I would have run into him. I mean, I'm very glad I haven't. No complaints here."

He nods, "I've hardly seen that guy since I arrived."

"Lucky you," I murmur under my breath, taking a seat. Asher slides into his seat across from me, waving hello at the other guests, before turning his attention back to me.

He screws his face up and leans forward on the table. "Did something happen with Sawyer?" He asks suspiciously.

I shake my head, laughing softly. "Nothing happened, I promise. He's just awful, a real grump. I'm glad he has been keeping to himself."

He looks as though he doesn't believe me, but he lets it slide.

After dinner, we wander through the inn, and I show him some of the other rooms. The sitting room is situated by the front door and has the perfect reading chair by the window. It also has a deep window seat that can easily fit two people, and I imagine us lazing there together.

Asher must catch on because he points at the window. "Maybe tomorrow you can read by that window, and I can catch up on finishing the lyrics to my new song. The studio is on my back to get them done."

"I would love that."

Chapter 11

AFTER WE DO A COMPLETE tour of the downstairs, we wander upstairs to take a look around. Pearl stopped us on the way up to let us know that she has a bread-and-butter pudding for dessert, and it will be ready in ten minutes. She winks as she says it, and my suspicions are piqued.

It's my favourite dessert. I look at Asher as she disappears and he smiles coyly.

"Did you tell Pearl…"

He leans back against the wall of the stairs, letting one of the guests pass.

"Yeah Peaches, I did. It was always your favourite dessert at Christmas. I didn't want you to miss out on having it and after I saw the menu for the week, I asked Pearl if she could add it in. She was more than happy to."

Acts of service have always been one of my love languages and Asher has always filled my cup in that way.

My chest feels warm, emotions bubbling up inside that make me teary.

My head drops and I blink fast, hoping the tears won't fall.

His hand tucks my hair behind my ear, and I look up at him as a single tear, escapes down my cheek.

Before he can say anything, I'm quick to reassure him. "I'm fine, I promise. These are happy tears. I swear."

He steps closer and takes my hand, kissing my palm.

I hear a door close upstairs, and I jump back.

"Hey, don't worry about any of them. Just worry about us."

Us. Is there an us? It feels a lot like we are playing with fire, between what we want and what's realistic for our lives.

He kisses my cheek softly and I take a step back, his hand falling from mine.

"What is this?" I blurt. I gesture between him and I. "Between us I mean."

He takes my hand in his again, his thumb rubbing over the back of my hand.

"I know what I want it to be peaches… what I've always wanted it to be. I'm not sure what you want it to be though?"

I take in a deep breath. Time to be brave.

But the words that tumble from my mouth come out all wrong and I'm kicking myself after.

"No one could know."

He winces, surprise flashing on his face and he swallows deeply.

Shit, that's not what I meant. I didn't mean to say… I wish I had chosen other words.

But before I can say anything else, explain it more, a door at the top of the stairs, swings open and Lorenzo emerges. I drop his hand and take the next step up, creating a little distance between us.

He looks devastated, before his face turns to steel.

I realise then, it must look as if I'm embarrassed of him. When that's the furthest thing from the truth.

I mumble a hello to Lorenzo, before turning back to Asher once he is out of sight.

Now it's his turn to take a step back.

"You know what. I'm not really that hungry. I think I'm going to skip dessert."

His expression is grim, before it closes off. He heads up towards his room and my mouth opens to say something, any-thing, but no words come out.

I trail along behind him, hoping I can find the right words to fix this.

He reaches his door, turning the key in the lock.

"Wait, Asher." I can hear the desperation in my voice, and he must too, because his hand stops, resting on the doorknob. He slowly turns towards me, waiting. Almost like he's ready to take off at any moment.

"I didn't mean… what I just said, it came out wrong. I don't want to hide you. Not forever. I just have to for a little bit. I…" He shakes his head and turns the handle.

"Goodnight Cassidy," he mutters, before stepping out of sight and closing the door behind him.

I stand there in shock at what just happened, before finally opening my door, my own appetite for my favourite dessert, suddenly gone.

A loud knock at my door, wakes me. I sit up, my heart pounding and a quick look at the window tells me it's night. I must have fallen asleep when I laid down earlier.

I spent the first hour laying here thinking about what happened in the hall and how happy he looked before I went and ruined everything.

A knock sounds again, hollow against the wooden door. I slide off the bed, catching the time on the clock. It's 9pm.

Another knock sounds and I hurry off the bed, the carpet soft beneath my feet as they sink in with each step. I inch the door open slowly.

It's Asher.

I open the door a little wider and wave him. His expression is pained yet he steps in confidently through the door.

I push it closed behind me, not wanting to make it easier for him to just leave.

I need to apologise.

But before I can say anything, he gets in first. "I'm sorry… I didn't give you a chance to explain anything earlier. I was too hurt. I still am. But I want to hear what you didn't get to say earlier. If you still want to say it."

I squeeze my hands together tightly at my chest, nerves getting the better of me.

"Yes, can we sit? I think I can explain better if I don't feel like you're about to run out of here."

"I'm not going to run again Peaches. I want to understand."

I wander over to the chairs by the window, hoping he will follow me. He does, thankfully.

We take the seats opposite each other, and I tuck my feet up underneath me.

I see his eyes follow my every move, the flash of heat in them making me lose my train of thought.

I clear my throat. "So… I meant what I said but not how I said it. And definitely not the part where I hurt you. That's the last thing I would ever want to do."

He rests his forearms loosely on his legs, leaning forward with that intense gaze he is well known for. And right now, it's aimed at me.

"So, tell me exactly what it is that you want Cassidy."

I hate conversations like this. I shy away from them whenever I can. But this is the person I've felt I could be most vulnerable with in the past and by all accounts, he seems to be that same person still.

"I want you. It doesn't make sense to my logical brain to be saying that after just a few days. But I don't want to go another seventeen years without seeing you, and I don't want to waste any more time." He doesn't move a muscle, watching me carefully.

"What's the catch here Cassidy? Because you said before no one can know, and that's a pretty big catch in my books."

He's right. But it's one condition I have to stick to. "I'm up for a big promotion at work. Huge promotion. I feel like I've worked my whole life just for this one. But. My boss is unashamedly a huge fan of yours. For years he has openly talked about going to your concerts, your latest song releases and everything in between. It's crazy. Every year we all chip in and buy him tickets to your show. That's how much of a fan he is."

Asher nods but still looks puzzled.

"Okay… so he's a diehard fan. I don't want to sound conceited, but lots of people are Peaches."

He stares at me expectantly and I shake my head, leaning forward in my chair.

"Asher, I'm going to get that promotion. I've worked my butt off for it and I know I deserve it. If we go public, and let's be real, everything you do becomes public, he will find out. And then when I get that promotion, everyone is going to say it was because of you. They'll know deep down that it's not, but jealousy is a hard pill to swallow. And once that rumour starts, it won't be contained and that will follow me everywhere I go. Every new project or research that I'm part of, will be tainted with that brush. It will ruin my work's credibility. I can't have that happen. For me or for my work."

Understanding slowly dawns on his face, the more I speak, and he nods slowly.

"Okay. I might not fucking like it, but I understand what you mean now. So how do we do this then?"

He rubs at the back of his head and takes a deep breath, before tilting his head to the side and adding. "I would never want to jeopardise your career. You know that better than anyone. You tell me what we need to do, and we'll do it."

He takes my hand in his squeezing it lightly before turning it over and tracing a path over the lines on my palm and I'm reminded of the psychic fortune teller again.

"I think we need to just keep this under wraps for now. Just till maybe early into the new year. I'm expecting the promotion to come up in January. I just need a few months. That's it. And then we can stop hiding this…" and I gesture between us.

I'm a bubbling mess of nerves inside, thinking about having to face scrutiny from the general public. Could I really handle that this time?

I don't have the answer to that question. But I know he's worth trying for.

His mouth curls up into a small smile. "I can do that. A few months is nothing, if it means I get to have you back." He leans forward and effortlessly lifts me from my chair, placing me on his lap.

I instantly curl in, wrapping my arms around his shoulders and resting my head on his chest, breathing him in. He dips his head, his lips finding mine, his tongue gently teasing mine open. His hand slides up my arm and over my shoulders and neck, cupping the back of my head.

A loud crack on the window scares the crap out of me, and I jump back almost falling to the floor. Asher catches me before I tumble backwards and I look to the window, expecting to see a crack in the glass.

All I see is powdery snow. I jump up and peer out the window, watching as a snowball sails through the sky and hits the window again.

Asher jumps up this time and opens the window, searching for the culprit. Another comes soaring through the air and he slams the window shut just in time.

A grin settles on my face when I spot the perp. I point towards a group of kids on the other side of the fence, all laughing and racing away, hiding behind the large oak trees. The home on the other side of the fence looks to be just as old as this one and has been renovated too. There is a huge treehouse in one of the trees, the kind that every kid dreams of. It reminds me of the one I had when I was little. Smoke plumes out of the chimney and I imagine the inside is just as cosy and warm, as the inn.

I spy one of the kids peeking out from behind a tree, a huge grin covering their face and I break out into a fit of giggles. Asher turns, leaning back against the window ledge, smiling wide.

"My favourite sound in the world."

I squint at him, a little confused, but still smiling. "What is?"

"You laughing Peaches."

Chapter 12

LATER THAT AFTERNOON WE TAKE another walk around the property. I don't mind that we can't go far due to the snowstorm. Each time we wander around the inn's yard, I see something else to marvel over. A deer and its fawn making their way up to the fence line, a squirrel in the tree looking for some food or even just admiring over the frozen lake at the back of the property.

I watch as Ted and Esme, attempt to skate across its icy surface. They are laughing as they cling onto each other, trying to stay on their feet. They must be in their late sixties, but they laugh and tumble as if they are much younger.

It's beautiful to watch.

I add it to my list of things we need to do while we are here.

We are just on our second lap, when I spot the kids from earlier, the snowball bandits, on the other side of the fence.

There are three of them and they are making a snowman together. I nudge Asher, pointing over at them silently, before quickly pulling us behind a tree.

His chest collides with mine and for a moment I forget what I was about to suggest.

He must mistake my intention, because he rests his arm against the tree above me and leans in for a slow and fiery kiss that warms me, in spite of the cold. I get caught up in the kiss before remembering why I pulled him behind the tree in the first place.

I pull back laughing and put my finger to my lips.

I whisper, "Those kids from earlier, the ones that threw the snowballs. They are just over that fence."

I raise my eyebrows a few times giving him a huge smile.

The confusion on his face disappears when he connects the dots.

"Hmmm seems like it might be time for a little light-hearted payback."

He takes my hand and we creep over to the fence line, hiding behind a large bush, where we fall to our knees in the snow. I notice then that there's a small fence gate between the two properties and it looks well worn. It must get used often.

We work quickly, forming small snowballs that are so light they will disintegrate when they hit their target.

"Ready?" I nod eagerly, ready for a snow fight.

"Now!"

We jump up, unable to control our laughter as we half crash into each other, alerting our victims to what's coming next.

The kids turn to face us just in time for the first hit of snowballs.

They shriek with their own laughter and run, hiding behind trees, likely readying their own snowballs.

I drop to the ground again and start making more. When I pop back up, I see snowballs sailing through the air towards us. Towards me more specifically.

Asher grabs me by the waist and in a fit of laughter, we dive the ground. He leans over the top of me, shielding the back of my head with his hand, from the snow beneath me.

My body is frozen, but I can hardly feel the cold wet seeping in through my clothes.

I don't care right now. I'm having too much fun.

I peck him on the lips before sitting back up and discreetly rolling a bigger snowball, while he works on the softer, smaller ones for our little targets next door.

When Asher isn't looking, I raise it in the air, ready to launch it at him. He turns just as it makes its way towards him and ducks.

Damnit!

But it definitely hits someone.

Sawyer. Shit.

"Oh, you've done it now. You hit the angry guy," yells one of the kids.

I haven't seen him in almost two days and here he is now, in the wrong place at the wrong time.

He slowly wipes the snow off his face, his eyes widening, steam practically pouring from his nose. The expression he gives me would turn snow into a puddle in seconds.

"You," he growls, pointing his finger.

Asher stands slowly and steps between us, blocking me. I duck around him, feeling surprisingly brave and bold, ready to defend my actions. From back here anyway.

"You… you… awful," he splutters before Asher cuts him off.

His tone is steel, strong and firm, unbending.

"Whatever you were about to say, don't. You won't speak to her like that. Or at all from now on. It was an accident. The snowball was intended for me."

Silence stretches between the three of us, and Sawyer's face reddens with anger. He glares at us both before storming off, back into the house, muttering angry words under his breath.

Asher shakes his head, only moving when the door slams shut and he's out of our sight.

"Wow, he really is pleasant isn't he," he says, that steel still lacing his voice.

"Yep, sure is. He mostly stays in his room, which suits me fine. Hopefully this deters him from coming out of his room again. And thanks for defending my honour," I say teasingly.

"Come here you menace," he drawls, grabbing my waist and pulling me close, planting a kiss on my forehead.

I'm hit on the back by a hard, wet object. Snowballs.

We get pummelled as we race to duck behind the closest tree, the moment with Sawyer all but forgotten.

The snow fight continues for a good half hour and ends with us finally conceding defeat.

Asher and I are too out of practice. And all of us, including the kids are covered in snow.

A worried voice rings out from behind us. "Oh, my goodness, kids! What did you do?"

It's Pearl. I turn to reassure her that everything is okay, but the kids beat me to it.

"They started it nanna!" One of the kids calls out. Tattletale.

"It was all in good fun!" Sings out another.

Asher chimes in, "I'm sorry Pearl. We did start the snowball fight. This time anyway," he mutters at the end.

She narrows her eyes, and turns to face them accusingly, hands on her hips.

"Kids, you're very lucky Asher and Cassidy don't seem to mind. These are our guests and what's the rule for guests?"

"Don't bother the guests," they all say in unison, sounding dejected.

I could laugh at the look on their faces at her scolding, which could barely even be considered a 'scolding'. But I do feel bad.

"It's really okay, Pearl. We were all having a great time."

She softens her gaze. "Okay, well don't think I don't know about the snowball to the window and who the culprit was. Be respectful to our guests," she says one final time before pulling them each in for a hug and disappearing back into the house.

I clap my hands together not ready for the fun to end.

"Who wants to make snowmen?" A cheer rings out from the kids, and Asher gives me the most light-hearted grin, I've seen since he arrived.

We spend the afternoon alternating between making snow angels and snowmen and while we work together on our creations, we learn that the three kids are Pearl and Dusty's grandchildren.

Their daughter is a single mum, so they are often at Pearl's place when she's at work.

Hence the well-worn gate between the two properties. There's Birdie, the youngest who's five, Sage the middle child who's eight, and Willis the oldest who is twelve. They are adorable.

Afterwards, Pearl ushers us all up to the verandah for hot cocoa and fresh cookies.

We sit with the kids by the outdoor fireplace and warm our hands. The kids talk a mile a minute, each vying for our attention, spilling stories about each other, their parents and Pearl and Dusty.

They are hilarious. And they make me want to meet their mum too.

Pearl pats my hand as she heads back in.

"Thank you dear. They look like they have had such a fun afternoon," she says smiling warmly at me.

I return her smile, telling her genuinely, "I had just as much fun, so no need to thank me."

Her smile twinkles again and she heads back inside, leaving us to all chat about who's snowman was best and who did the neatest snow angel.

An unfamiliar voice rings out, "Bird, Wills, Sagey! Are you guys over at nanna's?"

The wooden gate between the two properties swings open, and a woman similar in age to me, walks over, before jogging up the stairs.

She glances around at all of us, looking a little perplexed, but her smile is genuine and warm.

And for some reason, I feel instantly at ease with her, which hardly ever happens. My family is always telling me I need to make more friends but it's something I've always struggled with.

I stand, holding out my hand. "Hi, I'm Cassidy. We kind of started a snowball fight with your kids. I'm sorry," I say bashfully.

The kids break out into chatter, all at once, filling her in on their afternoon.

She raises her eyebrows and gives me the same twinkly smile Pearl gave me.

"It sounds like a wonderful afternoon. I wish I could have joined you all."

She glances past my shoulder, only now noticing Asher, and the warm smile drops off her face, replaced by one of shock.

"Holy hell… Asher Mills…" she whispers, her voice strangled.

He nods, an easy and friendly expression he reserves for people he doesn't know and for his fans, crossing his face. He holds out his hand.

"Hi, I'm Asher. I hope it was okay that we spent some time with your kids. They are really great. A lot of fun and they throw a mean snowball," he says with a big smile.

She nods, speechless. It's so interesting watching their exchange. I never got to see Asher's big rise to fame at its peak, and how his fans react to him in person.

Suddenly she laughs, her hands cupping her reddened cheeks. "I'm so sorry. I'm totally fan girling here, what an idiot. I just did not expect an international rockstar to be staying in my parents humble little inn. I'm Tabitha." She shakes his hand in return, laughing at herself again.

He puts her at ease instantly. "I couldn't have picked a better place to be snowed in. Their inn is amazing. I think it's my best Christmas ever."

He winks at me, looking all tender and sweet and I blush.

Tabitha looks between us with a knowing smile. "Thank you for being so kind to my kids. We are going to head home for some dinner and a nice warm bath. Thanks again," and she gives us both a kind smile and a wave.

I like her a lot.

Ashers hand slips into mine. "That was a fun afternoon."

I squeeze his hand in return. "So fun. I really needed that. Work and life have been… hectic. Who would have thought a snow fight would ease some of that stress."

He dips his chin in agreeance. "Me too Peaches. I hadn't realised how full on the tour was until I stopped. I'm in the best shape of my life, but I'm still so tired. I think this intense form of touring is coming to an end for me. The guys and I can see ourselves settling in to do more time in the studio, over the big tours."

His words hit a cord. Could his days of touring less, mean a better shot at long distance for us? I weigh it up in my mind, but I don't say anything. I don't want to influence any decision he makes regarding his career.

For me, the thought of a family has begun to cross my mind, more and more. Until now, my biggest priority was always work. But the last year or so, has had me wondering if a family could be in my cards someday too.

I think back to earlier in the snow. Asher was so good with the kids, and I could picture him playing with his own. Teaching them how to build a snowman, play the guitar, paint.

The words tumble from my mouth before I can stop them.

"Do you want kids? We uh, never spoke about that before… when we were younger."

His eyes widen slightly before his smile turns affectionate. His voice is soft but strong and sure when he speaks, and it does things to me that I never thought a voice could do.

"Yeah Peaches. I would love kids. Do you want kids?" He sounds hopeful but also hesitant and I can understand why. I've always been so career driven and I am in line for a promotion. I've made it very clear that there is a lot of work in the near future for me.

"Yes. I want kids. It was always something I saw for myself, but my career ambitions took centre stage for the longest time. But now I believe I could find a way to manage both."

At least, I hope I can.

A thoughtful look lights his face. "I never found anyone I wanted to have kids with… after you Cass. And so, I just took it off the cards. But my nieces and nephews have changed my mind about that. I love kids. And I would love my own."

His words hang in the air, giving me hope to cling to.

Chapter 13

Our cosy little bubble here at the inn is about to pop, the nearer we get to Christmas day.

And I am nowhere near ready for that.

My original plan was to see my family for Christmas, but what if we just stayed here… and I saw them a few days after Christmas, when Asher is due to return to work?

The thought continues to plague my mind, and I can't shake it. I feel guilty for ditching my original plan… but I really want to stay here.

With him.

Just after dinner that evening, I excuse myself to find Pearl in the foyer, doing some admin on the computer.

I leave Asher in the dining room, at the mercy of Dusty who has a bunch of questions about his time touring with another famous band that I've never heard of. They were both horrified when I told them that. As far as bands go, the only one I've followed all these years, has been his.

Pearl looks up from her computer with that sunny smile of hers and I muse to myself that she has become my honorary grandmother.

"Hi honey, what can I do for you?"

I run my hands along the edge of the bench, suddenly nervous.

Am I really doing this? Yes, I am.

"I was wondering if you have vacancies for Christmas Day and the few days after?"

Her expression becomes one of concern, and she walks around the bench, stopping in front of me, pulling me in for a hug.

"Oh honey, I'm sorry. I know you wanted to spend Christmas day with your family. All weather reports are saying that snow fall will worsen later tonight but then should start to improve tomorrow. We are hopeful the roads will reopen by Christmas Eve. But don't worry, if that doesn't happen, the room is yours. Our other guests cancelled when it snowed in."

I consider her words, wondering if I even tell her what I'm thinking. The room is free anyway, which gives me more time to think it over.

But I don't want to. I know my family will understand and I can see them a few days after Christmas.

It's worth it, I decide then and there.

A voice clears behind me, and I look over my shoulder at Asher, who's leaning against the doorframe.

"Cass, I'll find a way to get you home for Christmas. Even if I have to charter a helicopter somehow. I promise you I'll find a way."

If I didn't already love him, I would certainly love him for that.

"Thank you, Asher. But…" and before I finish, I turn back to Pearl.

"I was actually considering staying a bit longer, regardless of the roads… if it's an option?"

Judging from the look on her face, I've surprised her.

"Oh, well yes of course honey. The room is yours whatever you decide." She pats my arm before leaving the room and I spin around to face Asher, hoping it's joy and not disappointment on his face.

I'm rewarded with a wide smile. He pushes off the doorframe, striding towards me, taking my hand and gently pulling me towards him.

"Peaches, you want to spend Christmas with me?"

"Yes. But wait. Do you? I've been so caught up in my own plans that I forgot that you came back for Christmas too. Oh, I'm sorry. Just forget this conversation happened."

He shakes his head, "Hey, no. I want to spend Christmas with you. I see my family often. They travel out to see me, and I get back here once every now and again. If I called them right now and told them about us, they would tell me to stay. And

I want to Peaches. I want to wake up with you, for as many days as you'll let me, before we have to go back to our lives."

Excitement bubbles up in my stomach, thinking of spending Christmas with him.

Christmas was our favourite holiday together and his infectiousness for it, matches my own.

He rubs at his chin. "But I also don't want to stop you from seeing your family for Christmas like your dick ex. You came all this way to see them. That matters to me. What if we went and saw them together?"

That thought hadn't even crossed my mind and while I like that idea, I also love the idea of staying here, just the two of us. Holed up in this adorable Christmas inn. I'm not ready for our little bubble to pop… just yet.

"I guess… this year… feels like it's just for us?" I say nervously.

"Yeah Peaches. This feels like it's just for us."

Pearl sings out from the door into the living room. "I'm so sorry to interrupt sweets, but we are ready for you Asher."

I screw my nose up and he taps it lightly. "What's going on?"

Instead of answering, he wraps his arm around my shoulders and walks me into the living room, smiling wide.

The lights are off, and candles are lit, scattered around the room across tables and on the fireplace mantel. The sofas have been arranged in a U shape and the other guests of the inn, except for Sawyer, are all seated.

There's a single chair next to the fireplace and Ashers guitar is resting against it.

The fireplace roars behind him, the warmth filtering out through the room. Pearl walks in behind us, pouring cups of warm apple cider and placing a tray of hot cinnamon cookies, on the small table in front of the sofas.

The other guests all have blankets resting on their laps and when Asher leads me to a seat, Pearl quickly places one on my lap too. I dutifully tuck my legs under me, and Asher gives me a tender, intimate smile and my stomach fills with butterflies.

Looks like we are about to get a private concert.

I grin like a Cheshire cat, overcome with all of the emotions, my chest warm and tingly. It hits me then, that I'm the happiest I've been in a long time.

He picks up the guitar and plays a few test notes and I'm mesmerised already.

During the time we were living together, he played for me most nights. It was heaven.

I never realised just how much joy his music brought me and how much it filled our home, until it was gone, and it was suddenly always quiet.

"Good evening, folks, thanks for allowing me to play you some songs tonight. This first song is called 'The Slow Down'." He plays a few cords of one of his softer songs, his voice soothing the air, an electric charge coursing through the room as he sings.

He looks at me as he sings about a love rekindled and then reimagined, and I'm lost in his song.

Goosebumps sprinkle my arms and without even realising I've done it, I'm leaning forward, elbows on my knees, entirely captivated by his voice.

He sings a few more songs and I glance around the room, noticing it's not just me that is enchanted by him.

Everyone is wide eyed and lost in his song. I spy Margaret blinking back tears and Bill kissing the back of her hand. Pearl and Dusty are cosied up next to each other on another sofa. Everyone breaks out into loud applause when he ends the night, and my humble Asher looks at ease, but a little embarrassed. He gives everyone a small wave.

"Thanks guys, I appreciate the love. It's a blessing every day to do something I love and to share it with others. To share it with someone I love." His gaze burns into mine and I forget about everyone else in the room and that we are keeping this thing between us, under wraps.

Dusty thanks Asher for agreeing to do an intimate concert at their request, but I only half hear what he is saying.

Everyone trails out, thanking him profusely and before I know it, we are alone.

He places his guitar down gently before moving towards me, holding out his hand, slipping mine into his, before lifting me to my feet.

He places my hand on his chest, walking backwards until we stop abruptly.

"What did you think of the show Peaches?" I smile coyly at him.

"Fishing for compliments Asher?" His head tilts back as he roars with laughter.

"Always from you Cassidy. Always." He then points up at the ceiling, and I glance up in confusion, my gaze following his finger.

Mistletoe. Ah.

"It's only right we make use of this. I think it's illegal or something to not, isn't it?" He winks at me, and I feel my face warm.

I nod seriously. "Oh absolutely. Definitely illegal. But I would hate for you, to have to live up to a bad boy rockstar image."

"I'm in need of some street cred, so maybe I should just go then," he points towards the door with a cheeky smile, taking a step in that direction. I grab his arm, pulling him back towards, so close I can feel his breath tickling my cheek.

"Uh uh. Sorry my friend, but you're not going anywhere." I pull him by the collar even closer to me, my mouth finding his in a passionate kiss.

One that's a culmination of his sweet offer to get me home, his impromptu concert and everything from the last few days and seventeen years of missed moments, all rolled into one.

It's intoxicating and I moan into his mouth as his hand circles my hip, the other resting on the side of my neck.

We kiss like our lives depend on it, and I couldn't be more grateful for the mistletoe working its magic tonight.

Chapter 14

After Asher's impromptu concert and our kiss, he leaves me with a soft peck on the cheek, promising he will see me shortly.

He doesn't say where he's headed, and I just guess it must be work related. I have my own work to get done, but I just can't seem to muster the enthusiasm for it tonight.

I feel rested and relaxed for the first time, in a very long time. Maybe even years.

And I plan on savouring it.

I check my watch. It's still relatively early and I feel wired after watching him play. His voice fills every space he sings in, and he has an uncanny ability of settling right in your chest, making you feel warm and at ease.

I glance around the homely foyer, mentally ticking off all the rooms in the inn I could go to, instead of my own. I decide then to explore that cute little reading nook I saw earlier, by the front entrance and make my way there.

The room was small, probably once a mudroom, but the perfect size to tuck away with a book. I spot the cute little bookshelf, and I reach over to flick the lamp on.

Light floods the space, just enough to see everything clearly, but not so bright as to take away the cosy vibe of the room.

I scan the titles in wonder. The shelves are filled with so many gorgeous books. My fingers skim across the book spines, until I spy one of my favourites. Pride and Prejudice.

I gently pull it out, the heavy weight, a comfort in my hand.

I settle onto the cushions, in the window seat. The pale blue curtains are tied in cute little bows to the side of the window, so I have complete access to the view outside.

It's magical.

Fairy lights twinkle around the gazebo and more hang from trees around the frozen lake, lighting the hard ice.

Soft snowflakes trickle down from the sky, like a sun shower, gently coating the earth.

I can almost taste those snowflakes on my tongue. It was my favourite thing to do out in the snow as a child. My brother, sister and I would race around the backyard, throwing snowballs and building snowmen, much like the kids next door to the inn.

Maybe that's why I wanted to play with them. They remind me of my own wonderful childhood.

It's been so hard to not call my family the past few days, but I know if I do call, I'll get questions about working over the holidays, and I've never been a great liar.

I'm so lost in my thoughts I don't even hear Asher come into the room.

"A penny for your thoughts?" His husky voice echoes in the room, and I jump a little, my hand clutching at my chest.

"You scared me Asher… a little warning next time would be great." I try and slow my heartrate down and instead of looking remorseful, his grin widens.

"What was that noise you made just now? When I scared you. That was the cutest thing ever."

My cheeks warm and I shake my head.

"Nuh uh. There was no sound." I vehemently deny making it, knowing full well I definitely made a sound.

His hoarse chuckle brings goosebumps to the edge of my skin, and I wrap my cardigan around me even tighter.

I pat the cushion in front of me and in two strides he is there, taking a seat beside me. It's the perfect window seat for two, just as I had imagined it would be.

It's only then, that I notice he has something hanging from his hand. Two pairs of ice skates and my snow jacket.

Excitement bubbles up in my stomach and I sit up straighter, tossing my legs over the side of the seat, so they touch the ground again.

"Are we going ice skating?" I can hear the excitement in my voice.

I've not ice skated in close to a decade, and when I saw Ted and Esme the other night on the ice, I hoped I would get a chance to try out the lake before leaving the inn.

It looks like my wish is about to come true.

He drops the skates carefully to the ground, before moving to lean back against the cushions, crossing his arms. "I mean… I thought we would. But I can see I've interrupted you, so I'll go," he says with a playful grin on his face.

Asher makes to stand up and I pounce on him, grabbing his shoulders, the laughter bursting from me.

"No! You can't go. Please take me skating Asher. Please, please."

He chuckles again before kissing my nose and standing.

He holds his hand out and I slip mine into his, exhilarated at the thought of being out on the ice with him.

I pick up my own skates and snow jacket. "Race you!"

And I run from the room, through the foyer, before throwing open the front door, giggling as I descend the icy steps.

I slide on the last step and before I can hit my butt on the wood, a strong hand scoops under my arms, lifting me up.

Asher leans close to my ear whispering, "Easy tiger. You'll have plenty of time to slip over on that ice out there."

My head swings around to face him and I roll my eyes at him before scrunching up my nose. He throws his head back, roaring with infectious laughter and I join him.

"Come on you rascal, let's go skating." He holds his elbow out for me, and I link my arm through his, steadying myself on the slippery path.

I don't even care that there's a very strong possibility I'll slip over a thousand times tonight.

As we reach the edge of the frozen lake, Asher leads me carefully over to the bench seat.

He kneels at my feet, tenderly taking my boots off and replacing them with skates.

It's wild to me that this megastar rock god is on his knees, tying up my skates. Taking me ice skating.

He sits beside me, taking off his own boots and replacing them with skates.

"Where did you get these from?"

He plants a quick kiss on my cheek before standing and moving directly in front of me, both hands outstretched.

"Pearl. She keeps spares for the guests. And failing that, I would have been obscene and paid a helicopter to ship them in."

He grins sheepishly at that, and I remember that he made the same comment about a helicopter earlier this evening. It occurs to me then, that maybe he could have left much earlier than now, via said helicopter.

"Wait… so you could have left by now? In that fancy helicopter of yours?"

He scratches at his neck, sheepishly avoiding eye contact with me, as he walks me along the snowy path to the ice.

"Maybe… I mean they may not have been able to fly in anyway. But I also didn't ask either."

I read the hidden meaning in what he doesn't say and heat blooms in my chest.

He stayed here to be with me. I wrap my arms around him in an awkward side hug, careful to not trip us both over and he kisses the top of my head.

We reach the edge of the ice and for the first time, I notice how beautiful it really is out here.

Fairy lights are strewn across the trees that encircle the small frozen lake, lighting up the ice just enough that it makes the space feel romantic and intimate.

There's no one out here but us right now.

As my skate hits the ice, I wobble, and Asher grabs my arm, steadying me.

"I won't let you fall Peaches."

I know he won't. At least not while he is holding me.

"So that joke before, about me hitting the ice, wasn't you warning me you would let me drop?" I say teasingly, biting my lip.

"I would never drop you. Ever. And stop biting your lip, you're distracting me. I'm not going to be able to take you skating if you do that. Unless your intention really is to have me drag you back to the bedroom."

My heart pounds in my chest and I realise I'm holding my breath. When I exhale it's shaky, all the air leaving me. Up until this moment, I've been excited to go skating. Now, heading back to the bedroom instead, sounds pretty perfect to me.

I take a minute to admire the Asher standing in front of me.

His eyes sparkle in the glow of the fairy lights and he almost looks ethereal. Just otherworldly really.

His body is strong, and he towers over me in his skates.

His edgy look, the leather jacket and jeans, even compliments his ice skates.

He looks like the ultimate bad boy on ice. But the truth is, he's just a really freaking good guy under that tough exterior.

I let him pull me a few steps along the ice, as he skates backwards.

My skate slides out beneath me, and he quickly wraps one arm around me, balancing me while his hand cups the back of my head, tugging me close so he can rest his head on mine.

If my desire to skate around wasn't so strong, I would happily stay in this spot for longer.

But I'm already cold, unaccustomed to winters here after so long and I really need to move.

"Okay rockstar. Take me skating."

His laugh vibrates through his chest. "Let's do this. Show me what you've got Cassidy 'professional skater' Blake."

I roll my eyes, unable to hide the smile that threatens to spread all the way across my face.

He always teased me when we were teenagers about the fact that even though I grew up in snowy winters, I could not skate to save my life.

I punch him lightly on the arm before grabbing it again when I almost lose my footing once more.

He smirks at me. "Karma…?"

If I could get away with punching him again, I would. But I'd really rather not end up on my arse.

He slowly skates backwards, pulling me along. My legs turn out slightly, slipping and sliding every so often, like a newborn baby dear.

I don't know why I love skating so much when I'm just absolutely terrible at it, but I really do.

Asher stays strong and sturdy the whole time. He moves effortlessly on the ice, making this look so easy.

After skating around for five minutes with no more tumbles, he says, "Do you trust me, Peaches?"

Without hesitation or knowing why he is asking, I answer, "Absolutely."

We come to a stop, and he turns me slowly as if we are in a dance and he is spinning me.

But very carefully and slowly.

The familiarity of this move takes me all the way back to my teenage years. He stops spinning me when my back is flush with his chest. He moves his feet, so his skates are just outside of mine and he slowly moves us backwards.

Like it always was, when we did this move at sixteen and seventeen, my heart pounds, feeling as if it will explode any moment.

After a few laps, I feel my muscles begin to relax and it becomes soothing, this back and forth sway, Asher wrapped around me.

He was always a great skater. Growing up he was an ice hockey player and by the time I met him, he had quit.

But he loved skating. No matter how many times he spent coaching me on the ice, I never improved. It was laughable really.

My trip down memory lane is interrupted when two other skaters join us on the ice.

I notice then that there's a well-worn gate at the back of the property that is connected to a small dirt track, covered in snow. They must be locals who are welcome to use the lake when it's frozen.

Asher tenses when he spots them, watching them carefully before relaxing a little.

As we skate closer to them though, I notice them whispering and pointing.

Now that we are closer, I can see they are a young couple, no older than seventeen. But they are definitely pointing at us, and the young female is jumping up and down on her skates.

I take a moment to be impressed with her skill at being able to do that, before unease floods me.

Asher tucks his head close to mine and I realise then, as must he, that we have been spotted.

More to the point, Asher has been spotted.

"Time to go Peaches," he says skating us towards the bench.

But we aren't quick enough.

"Asher? Asher Mills? Oh my god, it really is you!" The young male calls out and I'm anxious to see how Asher wants to handle this.

"I'm such a huge fan of yours; I love Ash & Stone."

He turns to face them as they skate right up to us, and the worry melts from his expression.

They are so young and really adorable. I remember when we were young and adorable too.

"Hey, yeah I am. Think you can do me a favour guys?" Before he has barely finished, they are eagerly nodding, ready to do anything it would seem, from the look on their faces.

"No one knows I'm here, and I need to keep it that way. At least for a few days. Think you can keep my secret?" He charms them with that smile, but a quick peak at his face and I can see it's genuine. He truly does love his fans.

"Yes Asher, I mean Mr Mills. Sir," mumbles the young guy.

"Thanks guys, that means the world to me. I would really like to repay you for your kindness, so how about I leave two tickets with Pearl for my next concert. You can swing by and pick them up in a few days."

Their jaws drop and they silently nod. "Thank you, Asher Mills," the young girl whispers.

He gives them a wave, and we quickly skate off. We swap our skates for boots on the bench seat, before traipsing back along the path to the inn.

"Are you worried they will tell someone they saw you?"

He shakes his head, "Nah, I'm not worried. They won't tell anyone. They will probably be in shock for a few days, and those concert tickets will help them to stay quiet. For a little while anyway," he says with a huge grin.

I tuck in under his arm, fitting there perfectly.

"You big softy," I tease quietly, resting my cheek against his chest, as we walk.

"I am a big softy, Peaches. And how could I not be, when those kids remind me of us as teenagers."

"Young and hopelessly in love?" I giggle.

"Yes, that too. But mostly, two kids skating around a lake together with the world at their feet and the endless possibilities of a future together."

I hum my agreement, feeling a little sad at his description. We really did have the whole world at our feet back then.

"And if you didn't make the connection Peaches, tonight we were just two people skating around a lake together, with the world at our feet and endless possibilities for a future together."

Chapter 15

"Wake up Peaches. I want to show you something." I whimper, rolling away from him, swatting away his hand.

"It's too early and I'm on holidays. Holidays are for sleep ins Asher," I grumble, my voice muffled into the pillow.

He kisses a trail down my back and now I'm fully awake.

"It's good Peaches. You're going to love it."

He sounds really excited and it's so cute, that now I am too.

He has us rushing to get ready and I know that it must be good, when he knocks back my suggestion that we engage in some shower 'activities'.

He groans, running his hands down his face.

"You know I would never normally say no, and I really want to say yes right now but we don't have time."

He mumbles under his breath as I start putting my shoes on, "I hope this surprise is good because now all I can think about is that fucking shower."

I giggle, thoroughly enjoying seeing him squirm.

He takes my hand and leads me along the corridor, but instead of going down the main stairs, we continue past them and down another corridor to the left. We pass guest rooms, finally stopping at a room at the end of the hall.

Asher pulls out a key and fits it into the lock.

"Uh, where did you get that? And where are we going?" He shoots me a mischievous smile but doesn't answer my question.

We step into the room and immediately I spot a spiral staircase going up into the roof. I give him a curious stare before moving around the staircase, running my hands along its cool, wrought iron frame.

"This is beautiful. And it looks old."

Asher nods. "Yesterday when you slept in, I went downstairs to use the gym room. Pearl intercepted me and that's when she asked me to do the concert. But then she also told me about this room. And the one above." He points up at the ceiling and I'm intrigued.

"Are we allowed to be in here?" He dangles the key in front of me, chuckling.

"Of course, Peaches. I'm not a thug. I didn't steal this key. Pearl gave it to me when I told her just how much you would love to see it. It's locked because she doesn't allow guests up there. This lodge has been in her family since it was built one hundred and forty years ago. And what's upstairs is that old."

Okay, now I'm dying of curiosity.

"Can we go up?" I ask eagerly, my voice laced with excitement.

Kissing me chastely on the lips he points at the stairs. "After you ma'am," he says teasingly.

I try to contain my excitement and walk leisurely up the stairs. He steps close behind me, his lips tickling the shell of my ear.

"You want to run, don't you." I turn my head giving him a wide smile. "God yes."

He licks the shell of my ear and I'm instantly on fire. This man just needs to touch me, and I'm lit up.

Lightly slapping my butt, he laughs again.

"Go for it Peaches." I do as he suggests, not even holding back anymore, jogging as quickly as I can up the stairs, unprepared for what I find at the top.

I step out into a massive space, an attic, that covers the entirety of the size of the inn below.

It's enormous. But it's not the size that has me gasping. It's what it's filled with.

Books. As far as the eye can see.

It's a beautifully fitted out library, filled with shelves lining every wall, all the way up to the ceiling. The ceiling is a metre or so above my head, but because of the rooms size, it feels spacious in here.

There must be thousands of books in here. I breathe in deeply, the smell of old books settling in around me, like a comforting, old blanket. Beautiful velvet green sofas and reading chairs centre the room, a gorgeous and very old looking coffee table, placed in the middle.

Old and well-preserved reading lamps, adorn side tables and an incredibly large thick rug covers most of the floor. I can't even fathom how a rug could be that size.

Wooden floorboards, the same as the one's downstairs, cover the floor. I kick off my shoes by the door, not wanting to make any mess in here.

My bare feet pad over to the shelves to start inspecting books. I run my fingers along the spines softly, barely touching them for fear I will damage them.

Some of these books look as if they are close to two hundred years old. The room is very clean without a speck of dust. It must be used often.

I spin around, giggling, excited beyond belief.

"This is the library of my dreams! Remember we always talked about the one thing our home would need to have. A huge library."

I twirl around, my back to him, looking for my first book to pluck from the shelves. Asher grabs my waist, pulling me flush against him. He softly kisses my neck, resting his face there, his lips grazing my ear.

"We will have that. I promise you Peaches." Surprise flashes through me with his words. It might seem sudden to other people, but to us it's not really. It could never be sudden with us.

I feel giddy with his words. It's a promise of things to come and it warms and comforts my heart.

We spend the next few hours pulling out books and reading different excerpts to each other, lazing around on the sofas and then over at the desk by the large lamp, when we find something extraordinary.

My stomach starts to grumble, and I begrudgingly admit it's probably time to head down for lunch. Just as I'm about to concede, I hear the creak of the stairs.

Asher checks his watch, smiling. "Right on time."

He jumps up from his spot on the floor where he was leaning against the sofa, reading a poetry book and walks to the door. It swings open and there stands a beaming Dusty, holding a basket and a picnic blanket.

"Glad to see someone making use of this beautiful library. I'm always telling Pearl we should let our guests use it, but she says it's too special. I can see what she means, but it's nice to see faces in here other than our own. Enjoy," he says as he hands over the basket and blanket, before leaving.

"What's all this?" My voice is filled with wonder and a warmth spreads through my chest.

He moves over by the window, spreading the blanket out. "A picnic. I know you love picnics and it's not going to be too comfortable sitting on snow to enjoy one. I thought we could have one in here. Spend a bit more time in the library too."

My heart melts, just like the soft snow on the windowpane outside.

He remembered how much I love picnics. I almost have to pinch myself that we are sitting here in a dream library having a picnic by a snowy window.

I don't think my day could get any better.

Asher takes a seat on the blanket, reaching up to take my hand, pulling me down to sit by him. He takes out containers of ham sandwiches, potato salad, cheese, fruit, mince pies and sugar cookies.

He also pulls out a flask of homemade lemonade and it couldn't be more perfect. I brush at the corners of my eyes, where tears have started to pool.

"This is amazing Asher. This whole day, your thoughtfulness. I couldn't ask for anything more. Thank you," I all but whisper.

He flashes me that megawatt smile. "You know I would do anything to see you smile." My heart warms at his words, so grateful for this wonderful man.

Chapter 16

WE SPENT THE REMAINDER OF the day lazing in the library, picking at lunch leftovers and reading pages to each other.

I had no idea that's what my perfect date would be, but now the bar is set high.

I jokingly tell him that and he practically growls at me, telling me I won't be going on any other dates, with anyone else, in my future.

We skip dinner, feeling too full from grazing on our lunch, and after dropping back the key, we wander back to my room, ready to hibernate for the night.

I push the door open, and Asher wordlessly hands me a case that he pulls from the pocket inside his leather jacket.

"What's this? "A CD? I haven't seen one of these in years."

I turn it over and all it says is, 'For Cassidy'.

He points behind me to the table, and I turn, spotting a CD player.

"Pearl dropped one off for me while we were at the library."

I run my fingers along the edge of the disc's casing. It's well worn with a few cracks, and it looks old.

I look up at him shyly, feeling like this might be something important. He tips my chin up, softly stroking it, keeping my eyes on him.

"I'm serious about this. About what's between us Peaches. I've missed you more than I could ever put into words. But maybe this will help you to see how in this, I really am. I felt like I lost a huge part of me the day you drove off and I never got it back. Right now, it feels like I'm whole again."

I'm at a loss for words, for another time again this week. I would never have imagined this was how was my week was going to go.

"I don't ever want to go back to feeling that way Peaches. Like my heart was off walking around somewhere and I couldn't get it back. I was fucking lonely, for the longest time and it wasn't because I was alone. I was surrounded by people all the damn time." His voice grates, the frustration oozing from his words.

"I love my job, but I'll always love you more." He takes a deep breath, just as my own hitches. "I'm sorry I didn't show you that when you left. Who knows, things might have been different."

His eyes search mine before he adds, "I started recording this a long time ago… I want you to listen to it alone. I'll be next door when you're finished." His hand slides down my shoulder and arm before grabbing my hip.

He tugs me towards him, claiming me, his mouth urgent on mine.

And just as quick as our kiss, he lets go and he's gone, his door closing behind him.

I shakily take a step back, swinging my own door shut behind me.

He loves me. It's not a total surprise after all of the conversations we have been having, but it was still a pinch me moment.

I spin the case in my hand, rhythmically and almost absentmindedly, while thinking over his words.

This man, who could have anyone in this world, wants me. Me.

I still can't get over that and maybe I never will.

On stage, the world knows him as a magnetic, borderline cocky, presence. It's difficult to pry your eyes away from him, once you start watching.

But then away from that persona, to me… he's just Asher. Open, honest, thoughtful, fierce, loving, protective and strong, with a deep heart.

I move towards the CD player and pop it out of the case and into the allocated slot.

I close it and press play. I select track one and sit on the bed, tucking my legs up. Using a CD player takes me back to being a teenager. It's a nostalgic feeling hearing the sounds of the disc spinning as it loads.

The song starts with the slow, mellow sounds of an acoustic guitar. Then Asher's soulful voice floats through the room. It doesn't take me long to realise this isn't a rock song. It's a ballad.

An ode, a declaration to a love. It's beautiful.

To me. His voice croons and I shiver, feeling every one of his words, deep in my soul.

I feel alive, electrical nerve endings lighting up my skin.

At the end of the song, he records a few words.

"I miss you Cass. It's been a month and every day I want to leave this life behind and find you. But it's not just about what I want. It's what you wanted too. And I know how important your job is. But I'll love you for the rest of my life Peaches."

My chest tightens and I choke back a sob.

He wrote me a song. One that's never been released.

And it's all about our relationship and us.

The next song starts and ends with a few more words, similar to the first. I can hear the pain in his voice.

As each song plays, it hits me. There are seventeen tracks.

He has recorded a song for me, every year since we broke up. All private, none released to the public.

Seventeen tracks… wait. Seventeen? That means… the last recorded song was this year.

I reach the last song on the album, and he sings along with his guitar, a tune that sounds eerily familiar.

It's the song I heard through the wall, his first night at the inn. The song is about facing a life alone, not willing to give up the memory of us, just to be with someone else.

My heart aches at the pain in his voice. He has hidden it so well, all these years.

On stage he is dynamite, a force. His crowds go wild every time. But on this CD and in private with me, he is tender and soft. Loving. Vulnerable.

I wipe away a few errant tears and march to the door, with one mission in mind.

I race out into the hall and bang on his door, desperate to see him. As he opens the door, I throw myself at him, wrapping my arms around him tight and crushing my face into his chest.

His arms wrap around me too and he rests his head on top of mine.

A commotion rings out from downstairs.

"What's going on downstairs?" He sounds confused and I am too.

"I'm not sure. I was just coming to see you… to thank you. Actually no. That's a pathetic word for what you did. The gift you have given me. I…"

The front door of the inn closes with a loud bang, and more voices fill the foyer.

"We should probably go see what's going on," I say hesitantly.

"Asher and Cassidy! Are you both up there? We need some help down here."

We exchange a concerned glance before taking off for the stairs, rushing down them till we reach the entrance hall.

In the foyer, we find a worried Pearl and Dusty, Lorenzo, Alessandra, and Tabitha, who is wringing her hands as she paces.

"What's going on?" Asher demands his voice quiet but strong.

Tabitha covers her face and Pearl rubs her back.

Dusty's voice cracks. "Tabby's oldest, Willis, has gone missing and it's getting darker. They were all playing hide n seek in the garden a few hours ago and the youngest kids haven't seen him since. The neighbours are banding together to search around. Tabby's called a few of his friends, but no luck."

A look passes between us, and we silently agree to help.

"We will join the search. We grew up in the next town over and we can handle a search in the snow. Who do we speak to?"

Dusty tells us who to ask for on their front lawn and we stride out the door, to find one of their neighbours directing people where to go. They ask us to join the search in the woods at the back of the property. Asher and I head off into the woods, after securing a flashlight from Pearl.

"I doubt he's out here, but it can't hurt to check." Asher sounds worried and I am too.

We walk in silence, occasionally calling out his name, but it's quiet out here. After ten minutes we stop, taking a minute to regroup.

"Okay, so we need to think like a kid who's playing hide n seek. Where would we go?"

We throw a few ideas around but come up empty handed.

I start ticking off on my hand. "We need to look at the facts. He is twelve, playing with younger siblings. So, he isn't going to go far. Likely not off the property. Or even Pearl's property. Cubby house?"

He shakes his head. "They searched that."

"Hmm okay. Well, the majority of the search party are looking in Tabitha's property or over on the street. So those areas are covered. Have they looked at Pearl's property?"

Asher shrugs. "I overheard someone say they searched her property quickly, but that the kids aren't supposed to play hide n seek over here when there are guests."

"Well, it's got to be somewhere that's a good hiding spot that's not too far away. Despite what the neighbours said, it must be somewhere on the two properties for sure. The spot has to be sheltered because it's cold out. And it must be warm enough for him to not have come out of hiding by now."

I pray, anyway. I don't want to think anything bad.

Asher snaps his fingers, and something clicks in me. At the same time, we both shout, "Gazebo!"

We tear through the woods and into Pearl's backyard, past the verandah and around the side of the house, racing to the back corner where as expected, a small warm fire is burning.

We come to a sudden stop once we hit the top step and see Willis tucked in the corner, hidden from sight and laying on the bench seat with a big thick blanket over his body.

He looks warm and content and is fast asleep. I almost don't want to wake him, but I know we need to.

I shake his arm slightly. "Hey bud, you need to wake up." His eyes pop open and he sits up suddenly with a wide grin.

"Did I win Cassidy? I must have if you guys are finding me."

Asher chuckles. "You did win. But you also worried a lot of people, including your mum when they couldn't find you. Let's go find your mum buddy."

Chapter 17

WILLIS AT LEAST, HAS THE good graces to look sheepish at Asher's words and he shuffles along beside us back to the house.

As we round the corner, Tabitha spots us and bursts into tears, moving quickly down the stairs and lifting him up under his arms, embracing him.

Pearl and Dusty crowd us with thanks and Tabitha launches herself at us next, hugging us both.

"Oh my goodness, how can I ever repay you? That was the most terrifying night of my life. Thank God for both of you. Thank you, thank you."

We take turns hugging her before she walks off with a very remorseful Willis.

"You must both be frozen! That won't do. Head upstairs and have a hot shower and then come downstairs in your pyjamas for some supper in the living room." Pearl ushers us up the stairs, not taking no for an answer. I am cold, she's not wrong, and a shower and supper does sound wonderful.

I reach my door, turning to tell Asher I'll meet him back here in ten, when his hands bracket the door around me.

"Don't even bother telling me you will see me after a shower Peaches. I'm not going anywhere."

He turns the door handle, his other arm wrapping around my waist to stop me from falling as he walks us backwards, kicking the door closed behind him.

His hands travel down my hips and outer thighs, hoisting me up to his waist and I wrap my legs around him, as he presses his mouth to mine hungrily.

He rips my shirt off me, snapping open my bra and dropping that too, before walking us into the bathroom where he lifts me, placing me on the edge of the bench.

He is hurried in his movements, tilting my hips and sliding my pants and underwear down my legs, before dropping those to the floor, leaving me completely naked.

He steps back to look at me, taking me in, and I feel surprisingly comfortable with him appraising me. He stares at me in wonder, amazement crossing his face, looking at me like I'm the most special thing to him in the whole world.

This time when he steps closer, he is unhurried. He grips my thighs, running his hands up and down them, softly kissing my lips, before licking a trail down my neck, biting my collarbone gently.

"Let me warm you up in the shower."

He stands and kisses me lightly, his own lips soft. I suck on his bottom lip before gently biting it, his tongue licking my own, before he does the same in return to me.

I let him slide me off the bench, my legs wobbly when I hit the floor. He turns the shower tap on and gets the temperature right, before stripping out of his clothes.

I see firsthand how turned on he is, when he springs free from his pants, and I reach out to stroke it, earning an answering sigh of pleasure.

I step into the shower, and he follows, before closing the shower curtain behind him.

The space is small, but big enough that I can drop to my knees in front of him, the hot water pouring over us, as the steam fills the room.

I lightly run my fingers from his root to the wet tip, and he shudders, his hands moving to the shower wall to stay upright.

This time when my hand moves back down, I squeeze lightly and firm up my grip, pumping him up and down. My tongue darts out, licking the underside of him, all the way up to his tip. I take him in my mouth, as I pump him up and down with my hand. One of his hands grabs my ponytail gently, tilting my head back and watching as I suck hard. His eyes glaze over and he licks his lips.

"So fucking beautiful. But I need you up here with me Peaches. I need you to come undone on me again."

He pulls me up, his tongue pushing for entry and we kiss like we are making up for lost time. And we are.

He lifts one of my legs, wrapping it around his waist, plunging his fingers inside of me.

He's not gentle about it, remembering I've always liked him to not treat me like I'm breakable.

He pulls me closer, so our hips are touching and I reach between us, pulling his long length, squeezing at his base and gently stroking him.

He presses against me, and the friction sets off a warm buzz through my core. My back arches, my shoulders resting against the cool tiles, my breath hitching.

"Fuck I've dreamed about this Cass. Every damn day. Every night when I would shower, I would stroke myself imagining it was you doing it for me. And now you are. Fuck, I'm not going to last."

I lift my leg even higher and this time, I line him up at my entrance. He thrusts inside me and we both moan. "You're so beautiful Peaches. You're perfect. I love you." His words are hurried, breathless.

I try to murmur his words back to him, but I can't even speak, waves of my own orgasm building inside. His mouth sucks my nipple hard, and he swaps sides, almost tipping me over the edge from that alone. He rubs his two fingers in circles where we are connected and suddenly it's all consuming as I cry out, shattering around him.

He follows seconds later, shaking, his mouth finding my neck and kissing me everywhere he can reach.

"How very rockstar of us Asher," I murmur hoarsely, smiling. It feels like my bones are liquid.

His chest rumbles with a chuckle. "Maybe for other rockstars, but not this one. This rockstar is a one woman guy."

My hands circle his neck, and I rest my head on his chest, not even minding that my hair is getting soaked.

Asher turns me around and begins washing my hair and I melt under his hands.

Asher Mills takes care of the people he loves.

He starts lathering my body with the bar of soap. When his hands dip low, I moan.

"We've been in here for a while now. Pearl's expecting us. As much as I want to go again, we can't."

Asher groans into my shoulder, softly biting there before pulling the curtain open and helping me out.

As I step out of the shower, he peppers soft kisses across my back.

"I've got a pair of sweatpants and a tee in here that are clean I can wear. I'll borrow your complimentary slippers too Peaches," he says with a cheeky wink.

"The humble sweatpants and slippers for our gorgeous rock-star? I'm impressed," I tease.

He laughs, bright and loud and it warms my soul.

"I don't care what other people think Peaches. I really couldn't give a shit. The only person's opinion I've ever really cared about, is yours."

I falter, almost tripping over as I reach down for my towel to dry my hair.

"Oh. Well, that's nice," I mutter, embarrassed.

His eyes crinkle a little when he smiles at me. "It's the truth."

I dry my hair, lost in thought. It is the truth. I mean, I've always worried about what people thought of me, but I've only really cared about if he really saw me. And he always has.

Once we are dressed, we make our way down the hall, both of us in pyjamas and slippers. A warm, inviting smell of melted cheese wafts up the stairs.

We step into the living room to find the fireplace is roaring, the overhead lights are off, and the lamp in the corner is on.

The large fireplace gives off the most light into the room, bathing everything in a soft glow.

The table by the sofa, in front of the fireplace has two cups of tea, more of Pearls delightful cinnamon cookies and two grilled cheese sandwiches.

My mouth waters and I grab one of the sandwiches, biting into it, the cheese oozing out the side.

It's delicious.

Asher grabs one too and we kick off our slippers, settling in on the sofa. He grabs my legs and swings them up over his own, rubbing my feet with one hand while he eats his sandwich with the other.

We talk about the events of the night and laugh about our own teenage hide 'n' seek adventures. Except at the age of sixteen and seventeen, ours involved a lot of hiding and making out and not too much of the seeking.

"So… the CD. Wanna tell me about that?" I'm a mix of nervous and excited to hear his response.

He rubs his thumb over his bottom lip, and I can't take my eyes off the hypnotic movement.

"Well, shortly after you left, I thought about writing you a letter. But every time I put pen to paper, lyrics came out instead of sensical sentences. But then I realised, that's how I communicate best, through my songs. So, I started penning a love song to you. The first year I almost didn't record it, but then something clicked, and I worked out that I was never going to give up on us, entirely."

I sit in shocked silence, desperate to hear more and he doesn't disappoint.

"Early on, I thought maybe we would be apart for a few years. Just enough time to get our careers established and then I would find you. But then I followed your career, and you were soaring. And I realised that I couldn't make you give that up. And I wasn't sure I could give up mine either. So, I kept making the songs, hoping someday we would come back together when the timing worked out. I've carried the disc with me all these years, just on the off chance I could give it to you..."

My face is warm and flushed, a little from the fire, but also mostly from Asher's words.

The way he describes it, is exactly how his songs made me feel.

Like a love letter in the form of a song. His way.

I scoot over closer to him and take his hands in mine.

"I loved it Asher. It was perfect and perfectly you. I'm glad in some ways and definitely not in others, that you didn't send it to me. Because back then, I probably would have given my notice and come running back. But that wouldn't have been good for either of us. The more I think about it, the more I kind of like that it took us a long time to get here. To grow."

He tilts his head, leaning it against the cushioned sofa, looking as if he is considering my words.

"I have to ask Asher… did you really not know I was here? I mean, there's really no way you could have known. No one knew I was headed here, and I didn't even decide until last minute that I was going to come home."

"I had no idea, Peaches. I just knew I needed some family time and this Christmas turned out to be the one I could get off from work."

He rubs at his chin before he goes on. "When I realised I was snowed in, I had a choice to make. Two inns down the road or this one. I just knew it had to be this one. You always spoke about it, about wanting to stay here and there was no other choice. I like to think it was fate. You know I'm a hopeless romantic. It's turning out to be just like the movies. Some kind of big, serendipitous moment, right?" I laugh along with him, nodding at his words.

I think so too.

Chapter 18

Christmas Eve morning.

I stretch out in bed luxuriously, before Asher's hand snakes around my waist, pulling me in.

"You're too far away," says his muffled voice into the pillow. I grin into the blankets, entirely loving this clingy, affectionate side of him.

I let him pull me in, lifting my leg to tuck his under mine. I kiss his arm wrapped around me, trailing more kisses up and down.

"This is the way I want to wake up every day."

I murmur my agreement. I can't think of anything better. The snow has stopped falling overnight and I can see from where I lay on the bed, that the ground has thawed a little.

I sit up and point towards the road in the distance. The highway.

"Asher, it looks like the roads are open."

He murmurs something I can't understand, and I lay back down, curling into his embrace again.

It doesn't really matter to me anyway. We told Pearl last night that we would be staying on a few extra days.

Asher moved his bags into my room last night and I love the way they look piled onto the chair, his things mixed with my own.

I yawn again, my stomach growling.

"I'm starving. Let's get up and head down for breakfast."

He rolls onto his back, pulling me with him, nipping at my neck. "I'm good Peaches. I want to eat what I have right here." I laugh giddily as he nips across my collarbone and then back over to my neck.

The laughter dies from my lips when we are interrupted by the loud ding of my phone. It occurs to me then that my phone hasn't beeped in days. My family knows that this time of year is usually busy for me as I cover for my coworkers who are off with their young families.

I ignore it, assuming it's not important, but it sounds again. It's the third ding from my phone that has me thinking I should check it.

I roll to my side when a steady stream of notifications begins ringing out from both of our phones.

"What the hell?" Asher sits up, kicking off the blanket and reaching for his own phone.

My eyes scan over the screen. Messages and some missed calls from earlier when I was asleep, flash on the screen.

My hands are shaking when I unlock my phone and bring up messages from my sister, my brother and my parents. All along the same lines.

'You and Asher are back together!?' 'Holy hell that kiss is fire!' 'Cassidy, why didn't you tell us you were in the next town over? Your father and I are hurt we didn't know. Were you going to visit us at all?'

I can hear Asher swearing under his breath as he goes through his own text messages.

We turn to face each other on our respective sides of the bed. He looks stricken, worried.

I must look how I feel, when I see his brow furrowing.

Numb, freaked out, panicked.

Voice shaky, I whisper "What is everyone talking about Asher?"

He turns his phone so I can see the picture. It's Asher and I kissing under the mistletoe.

My hands shake as I take the phone from him.

There are another two photos of us where you can see that it's very clearly me, and very clearly him.

The last photo would be nice if the situation wasn't so shitty. We are laughing and leaning into each other. And we look very much in love.

But I feel gross, icky. Someone has invaded my privacy. Our privacy.

A thought flashes through my mind. This is what life must be like for him all the time.

And what my life will be like, with him.

"Where is it? Online? How have people seen these pictures? And who took them?" I scramble for words, the panic in my voice becoming even more pronounced.

His face darkens and he stands angrily, grabbing a pair of sweatpants out of his bag and pulling them on roughly. He grabs a grey tee and pulls that on over his head too.

I reach for my leggings and sweater, throwing them on haphazardly. He moves around to my side of the bed. and I fall into his arms, tears welling in my eyes.

"It was someone here obviously and I can take one guess who it might be." He spits.

I can too.

"Sawyer."

I feel his chest rise and fall fast.

"I'm sorry Cassidy. I'm used to this happening, but not to you. It's killing me seeing this affect you, knowing this has hurt you. What can I do to fix this?"

The numb feeling hasn't passed yet and I can't answer him right now, because I don't know what to say.

Surprising my parents is now ruined. Even though I'm here at the inn for Christmas, I still planned to surprise them in a few days.

Everyone is going to find out, if they haven't already.

My phone dings again and I grab it off the bedside, a glutton for punishment. I shouldn't even bother reading any more of the messages, but I do.

It's my ex, Felix.

His messages contain some expletives. A lot actually.

My face must give me away because wordlessly Asher takes my phone, his face hardening as he reads it.

"What the hell Cassidy. Is this your ex-boyfriend?" He is furious. He scrolls up further and I don't bother telling him to stop. I have nothing to hide from him.

His voice is steel, and I know he has read the other messages.

"Does he always speak to you like this?"

I shake my head. "Not before… and only a few times since we broke up. I told him to stop contacting me and he did. Until just now. I'm going to block his number."

He closes his eyes and takes in a few deep breaths. "I just need a minute. That message is… and I also need to have a word with our 'friend' who I'm very certain, is responsible for this."

He kisses my cheek and stalks out of the room, not even bothering to put on shoes.

Shit.

I slip my feet into my flats and race down the hallway, already hearing heated voices when I reach the top of the stairs. The voices echo through the room and up to where I stand.

I can tell Asher is restrained, holding back on saying and doing what he really wants to, likely out of respect for Pearl and Dusty.

"I know it was you. And I'll find a way to prove it Sawyer. You will regret ever posting those pictures."

I race down the stairs, and I'm greeted with an angry looking Pearl and Dusty, standing a few steps behind from Asher. Their frosty stares are aimed at Sawyer.

He sneers, but his voice wobbles a little when he speaks, giving away his nerves.

"Well, uh, it wasn't me. And even if it was, I can't get in trouble. This is a public place not a private residence. Maybe you should be 'kissing' somewhere a bit more private."

Oh geez. He didn't.

I can practically see the steam pour from Asher's ears and he takes a step towards him, just as Sawyer takes a giant step back.

The voice that speaks next isn't Ashers and it surprises the hell out of me.

"Well, it may not be a private residence, but it's our residence. And we asked everyone to be respectful of Mr Mills privacy while he was here. The roads are now open and it's time for you to go Sawyer."

Woah, Pearl.

I'm both grateful and stunned of her speech.

Sawyer's mouth gapes open like a fish, before he turns and marches up the stairs, complaining under his breath.

Pearl turns to face us, with tears in her eyes, "I'm so sorry to you both. If I had known, I would have done something earlier."

I lean in and give her a quick hug.

"You have nothing to be sorry for Pearl; it's not your fault. It's his."

She gives me a watery smile, and I pat her arm, wanting to stay and comfort her more but feeling teary myself.

I squeeze her arm once more and turn, giving Asher a quick, forced smile, that I know doesn't reach my eyes.

He takes my hand, and we make our way up the stairs and back to our room.

Just as I push the door open, my phone starts ringing and I rush to grab it. It's my boss.

"Umm hi, Jeremy."

He says hello back and then proceeds to tell me he has seen the post and is thrilled. He sounds ecstatic. He playfully scolds me for not telling him sooner about my new relationship. And then asks if I can get him VIP tickets, and if he can meet Asher, all in one excited breath. The final blow hits when he says cheerfully into the phone, "Of course you already know you will get the promotion, being the most qualified and all. But now, we could officially celebrate at their upcoming concert! The team is going to be so excited!"

No, they won't. They are going to suspect what I had worried about, the last few days.

That I got the promotion because of Asher. I can already hear the rumour mill starting and my hard-earned reputation, evaporating like dust. My heart sinks.

I politely cut the call short and promptly burst into tears when I disconnect.

"Hey, come here," Asher takes my hand and gently pulls me towards him, wrapping me in a warm hug. His hand rubs soothing circles over my back, as he kisses the top of my head.

"We can fix this. I will fix this. Let me call my agent and get it sorted. I'll find a way to get the pictures taken down before anyone else sees them."

Stepping back, I cross my arms.

"Asher, too many people already know. My boss knows. And he's probably the last person I wanted to find out right now. I know it's not your fault and I'm not angry at you, but I should have trusted my instincts. I should have been more careful. Just until the promotion at least. It's not just me that's affected, it's my work. I'm part of some huge lifesaving team projects right now and I need the complete trust and faith of my team to make these devices and therapeutic equipment, work effectively. We work very closely together. I can't have my team whispering about me or resenting me. Questioning my work."

He's nodding slowly but his expression turns more grave, the more I speak.

"So, what are you saying Cassidy?"

I draw in a deep breath. "I'm not saying anything right now… I just need some time. Alone. To sort this all out."

Chapter 19

ASHER SHAKES HIS HEAD. "No. I'm not letting you go this time. I just got you back. I can fix this. Let me fix it Peaches. Please."

My phone rings again and this time it's my colleague, Vera. I let it go to voicemail this time.

'Hey Cassidy, I just wanted to let you know that some of the senior team members who were up for the promotion too, are messaging the rest of us complaining that you will get the job now. And they have some of the junior members questioning whether it's true too. I'm sorry, it's a crappy thing. We all know you were going to get the job anyway. You're the absolute best of all of us. I just wanted you to know.'

A hot flush creeps up my body and I feel like I can't breathe in here.

I rush to the window and flick the latch, pushing it up and sticking my head out, taking in a gasping breath.

I watch as Sawyer carries his bag out to his car, glaring back up at the inn, like somehow, we have wronged him and not the other way around.

The small street is busy. Now that the roads are open, cars are leaving in large numbers, likely trying to get home to family or head out on holidays.

I know what I need to do, even if he won't like it. And I know he won't, because I hate it myself.

I step back, closing the window and turning to face him.

"Asher… this is escalating already, and I really need to get on top of this. I need some space to get it sorted… and to think. I know it sounds like it is, but this isn't a breakup I promise. I want to be with you. But it's just a minute's breather, to get everything back in order."

He's already shaking his head again.

I continue regardless. "We are so close to breaking through on this project. It would mean life changing devices for people worldwide. But I've seen petty shit ruin teams and projects fall apart from it. I'm so close. I have to repair this. And it's not a breakup." I reiterate.

"I respect what you're saying about your job, but the rest is bullshit Peaches. I'm sorry, but it is.

A 'break' is always a breakup."

"It's not. Have I ever been anything but honest and upfront with you?" He considers what I say for a minute.

"Well, you have always been honest… but this is sounding an awful lot like a fucking breakup," he says slowly.

He rubs at his eyes, and I can see how hard this is for him. How torn he is, wanting me to stay but also not wanting to force me.

I'm too numb right now to process what I'm even saying to him. I know later I'm going to be a mess.

But forcing each other isn't us.

His eyes are closed when he speaks again, as if he can't even look at me right now.

Between gritted teeth he says quietly, "Tell me what you need Cassidy."

Am I sure this is what I want? No. But I know it's what I need to do, even if it's going to tear me to shreds. I hate that I'm the project lead right now for a device that is in my sole area of expertise. If I wasn't, I would step down and let someone else in the team take over.

"I need to go back home. Just to think about a way to tackle this. It's not long term. Just till things blow over."

He turns away from me and I feel the chill in the air instantly. He moves to the other window, leaning against the frame, as he rests his head against his forearm and looks outside.

"How long is that? Because in my experience, things like this don't blow over in a few weeks. I'll get my agent to remove it, every minute it's up, is a lot more people who have eyes on it."

"I'm not sure… not long. I promise this isn't over. I don't want to lose you again. I just need a little time to work it out in a neutral space."

He nods, straightening, before walking back towards me and cupping my cheek, kissing me softly on the lips.

"I'm not going to lie Cass. This is crap. And I don't buy that it's not a breakup, but I can see your mind is made up and you're not going to change it. I just wish you had trusted me enough to stay and sort this out with me. Together."

The numb feeling from before is slowly thawing and big, awful emotions are settling in. I'm already finding it hard to breathe.

"I'm not going to watch you leave like last time. I don't think I could handle it. Let me know when you're ready to talk."

With that, he drops his hand and moves to the chair that holds his suitcase, tossing in a few things and closing it up. He doesn't look back as he picks it up and walks out the door.

I hear his door close quickly after.

The tears run unchecked down my cheeks, and I don't even bother wiping them away. They continue to pour from my eyes, lazily making their way down to my chin as I push through, packing my own bag, before it gets the best of me and I crumble to the floor. I sit there crying, wishing things could go back to earlier this morning, when we were blissful, before all of this happened.

Eventually I wipe my eyes and nose, doing my best to hide the fact that I've been crying. I swing my bag over my shoulder and close the door softly behind me, saying goodbye to a beautiful week.

I stare longingly at his door, a tiny part of me hoping he will burst through it and beg me to stay.

An unhelpful thought pops into my mind. What if, when I'm ready, he decides to not even take my call?

I reaffirm to myself that this is something I need to do alone. I've always done it alone and that's how I best operate through a difficult situation. Using my rational brain. And it works.

Well, mostly.

But it's also pretty freaking lonely doing it that way all the time. And why can't I do it a different way?

The thought gains momentum and it hits me then. I don't actually want to do it alone anymore.

What harm is there in trying it his way, together, and seeing if that works?

I drop my bag and rush to his door, banging on it. No answer.

I keep banging and calling out his name when I feel a soft hand touch my arm.

It's Pearl.

"Honey, he left about ten minutes ago. Said he needed some air and something about a repeat of history and he would be gone for the rest of the day. I'm sorry."

I give her a weak smile and brush the last trickle of tears off my cheek. "It's okay. It's actually for the best anyway. Please don't tell him I knocked at his door." She looks torn but nods reluctantly.

"Are you okay honey?" I shake my head but straighten, steeling myself like I've always done.

"I'm not, but I will be."

Chapter 20

THIS WAS ALL I WANTED this year. Christmas with my family.

And so far, it has been beautiful, at least on the outside. My whole family gathered around the dinner table, as my nieces and nephews play in the garden. Christmas songs and movies are the soundtrack for our day, while we drink eggnog and eat our roast dinner with the crispiest, most delicious, potatoes. I still don't understand how my mum gets them so crispy. They're so good.

But these festivities are missing something important. Asher.

As soon as I arrived late yesterday on Christmas eve, I fell into my mother's arms and burst into tears. I explained a little to them, enough that they could work out my heart is broken again.

I slotted right into family activities, but my parents have both given me enough sympathetic glances for me to know, I've not hidden my internal anguish, well enough.

I spent Christmas eve in fixing mode. I video conference with my team, choosing to be transparent about my relationship with Asher. I speak with my boss and let him know that I won't be able to connect Asher in any way to my work life.

Now, I just need to wait and see if that's enough.

I check online and true to his word, the pictures have all been removed.

After that, I put my phone down, telling myself I would be present with my family for the remainder of the holidays.

I do my best to get involved in the conversations and at the table that night while we eat dinner, the kids already ditching theirs in favour of playing with their new toys. It's just the six of us adults left at the table and I'm already wondering how I can excuse myself to go to my room and cry myself to sleep.

My brother Vance and sister-in-law Odessa are telling us a story about their recent holiday overseas and everyone is laughing. Mum is dishing out more food onto everyone's plates and my sister Marli, is asking questions about the trip.

I've missed this. And I was so looking forward to it, and now I can't seem to enjoy it.

While they are distracted, I glance around, studying everyone at the table.

They all look so happy, laughing at personal jokes and teasing each other.

My sister is single but happily so and always has been. Marli is my twin and while we look similar, we also have a lot of differences between us too.

Marli is a well accredited journalist and a social butterfly. Where I've struggled socially, she has flourished. I always joked that she has enough friends for the two of us.

Being around her makes me happy and she is one of the big reasons why I wanted to come home.

And now, I'm wasting it.

I need to pull myself together.

My dad rests his hands on my shoulders. "Are you okay honey?"

I smile up at him and nod, but here at home, I don't have to hide my true feelings and so my brave face doesn't last.

I burst into tears and concern etches his face, as he leans down to give me a hug.

"Oh dear," my mum says getting up to give me a hug too. I cry for a few minutes in their arms before pulling away and wiping my face.

They take their seats back at the table and now I'm faced with six, sympathetic faces.

"We know something happened with Asher, from the little you told us and the pictures we saw online, but we don't know exactly what. Do you want to talk about it?"

I shake my head before bursting into tears again. Before I can stop myself, the story pours from me, and I proceed to tell them everything that happened since I arrived at the inn… leaving out some parts that they don't need to know.

Marli leans over at one point and whispers to me, "I know you're keeping this PG, but you can tell Odessa and I the X rated parts later." She winks at me and Odessa, my sister-in-law, nods enthusiastically.

I can't stop the smile that crosses my face at that.

When I reach the end of my story, I take in a deep, shuddering breath. I feel like I barely came up for air the entire time.

Everyone stares at me in silence, and I can hear the loud echo of the clock on the wall.

My mum cracks first, giving me a warm, comforting smile. "Well honey…"

And before she can finish, my sister butts in. "You're an idiot. I mean that lovingly of course. You're an incredibly smart, accomplished leader. You can handle your team, their gossip or anything else that gets thrown your way. You're not being smart in this situation though. I get it. That guy at the inn is the worst and if you know his address, I will happily go and sort him out. But his stupidity is not a good enough reason to leave that fine man. Asher adores you! Don't throw that away on some random, awful guy's actions."

I stare at her in shock. Not at her delivery, but at her words.

"Marli, since when are you a romantic? I thought you hated relationships."

She screws her nose up and it's the cutest. "Well yeah, I don't love them for me. I haven't found anyone worth investing my time into. But you have. He's been your only love since you were sixteen. You guys have wasted enough time, don't you think?"

I'm still in shock when Vance speaks up.

"I agree. If I had to pick anyone that would be good enough for you Cassidy, it's Asher. Hands down every time. He's a good guy and he's always worshipped you. Did I ever tell you I ran into him in town? About three years ago. Wait, maybe it was four? Anyway, I ran into him."

I shake my head, not at all surprised. My brother is the most forgetful person I know. I'm surprised every year he makes it home for Christmas, but I know that's all Odessa's doing.

"He was home for Christmas and was buying some gifts in town. We ran into each other and ended up getting a beer together at the pub."

I'm floored. How on Earth did he forget to tell me about this? He just casually caught up with my ex, a world-renowned rock star, in town for a beer, and nothing was mentioned for four years.

Odessa looks annoyed and waves him on, to hurry and finish his story. I guess I'm not the only one who didn't know.

"Anyway, he asked how you were. He talked about all your achievements and how he had been following along with your career for years. He was proud. Really proud Cass. And then he said that you were the love of his life. He was a few beers in, so I wasn't sure if it was the alcohol talking. But he seemed like he meant it."

Odessa taps his arm lightly in frustration. "Why didn't you tell me this either?"

He shrugs, looking sheepish. "I'm sorry honey, I honestly forgot. I was shopping last minute, so I was probably in a rush.

And I think it was around the time you were with that guy, what's his name again?"

"And you didn't think I would want to know either?" I tamper down my frustration at my brother, knowing that's who he is, but upset all the same.

He looks remorseful and I instantly feel bad. He's one of the most caring and thoughtful people I know, and he wouldn't have done it intentionally.

And would it have mattered anyway?

"I'm sorry Cassidy. I really am. But don't waste this chance now. I mean the guy wrote you that famous song years ago. We all knew it was about you. I think you were the only one who didn't realise."

"Forever entwined. Yes, I know."

Marli shakes her head. "Not just that one, the other one too. The one that was even more popular."

"What song?" The frustration is clear in my voice.

Almost as if it was planned, everyone at the table sings in unison, "My world became dark and grey, I thought you were here to stay, why weren't you here to stay. Our song got lost along the way, and now I wonder if I'll ever get it back, if I'll ever get you back."

I look around at everyone, feeling only slightly betrayed.

"Why didn't you all tell me this? That you felt like this?" My voice is soaked in emotion, and I do my best to hold back the next wave of tears threatening to pour out.

Mum clears her throat. "Well, honey it's your life. Our feelings don't matter. And you and Asher showed such maturity at such a young age to walk away from something special, to pursue something that brought you joy. I knew then that whatever you chose, you were capable enough to make that choice. And to live with it, however you chose. But life changes and so do our hopes and wishes. I can't help but feel like this seems to be serendipitous. What are the chances you would meet at The Snowflake Inn?"

She's right. I know she is. What were the chances?

"There's more. I left something out."

They all stare at me expectantly and I breathe in deeply. "He wrote me a song every year we weren't together. He wrote me seventeen songs, each written around our anniversary," I blurt.

It's almost comical to watch their expressions change, from surprised to amazed, but they all settle on shock.

"Um excuse me? I don't think I heard you correctly. Because if I did, I would be wondering if you have lost it. Like truly lost it. Why are you still here talking to us when that man made you a personal play list!" I can't blame Marli for being incredulous.

The more I talk about him and this past week, the more I realise I am a huge idiot.

She must realise her comment was a little rough, because her approach is a touch softer this time. "Okay I'm not going to berate you anymore, because I can see how hard this already is for you. But please tell me you have the playlist, and we can listen to it?"

I chew at my lip, thinking about what Asher would want. Would he want everyone listening to his heart felt songs? He hasn't released them to the public for a reason.

I mentally replay the songs in my head, and one springs to mind that I know instantly he won't mind them listening to.

"I have one you can hear. But the rest are so… heartfelt and intimate. I'll keep those for me."

I pick up my phone and carefully select one song. Asher gave me the disc to keep but also transferred the album to my phone. It's clear it's been recorded in his own personal studio.

This one is slow, a yearning timbre echoing in his voice. He sings about a love so sweet it was worth moving mountains for. A love lost, that's worth draining the streams. It's beautiful.

I glance up as the song ends. No one has moved an inch. My sister wipes tears from the corner of her eyes and my dad doesn't even hide the tears that run down his face.

"Cass… you know how strong you are, right?" Marli says kindly. "You can handle anything that this life with Asher throws at you. You're not twenty-two-year-old Cassidy. You're a badass Biomedical Engineer who speaks at conferences, who creates life saving devices. Be that person."

"Sweetheart. What are you waiting for?" My dad asks.

What am, I waiting for?

Chapter 21

After dinner we carried on our night like nothing happened, for the most part.

But every so often, someone steals a glance at me. I'm not sure whether it's to judge me, pity me, or to make sure I'm okay. Probably a combination of all three.

While everyone watches Christmas movies, I get lost in my thoughts.

I told Asher I needed space and I wasn't sure for how long. It's only been a day and a half and that feels like too much space already.

I was so worried about being in the public eye, so scared to be scrutinised and worried for my work, that I let it sway my feelings and what I really want.

Which is him. It's always been him.

I think about what my sister said.

I couldn't handle the kind of fame he has now, back when I was twenty-two that's for sure. But she's right. Thirty-nine-year-old Cassidy Blake can.

I am so much stronger now. I have done the big conferences, and I have been scrutinised for my work by naysayers.

I can handle this. I have an overwhelming urge to call him right now and apologise.

I feel my resolve building, and I search through the house for my phone with no luck.

I just had it at dinner, so it must be somewhere nearby. I sing out "Has anyone seen my phone?" But all I get back is complete silence, everyone caught up in their own Christmas activities.

I'm just about to give up the search when I hear a cute little laugh. I spot two feet poking out from under the dining table.

I kneel down and laugh when I see who's under there. I crawl under, laying on my back too.

"Whatcha doing cutie?"

My niece Sera, who is eight, gives me a cheeky smile, hiding my phone a little closer to her face.

"Just playing a video game," she says giggling. I laugh too, not in the slightest bit angry with her for taking it.

She shows me the game she is playing, and I get so caught up in talking to her that I forget all about why I needed it for a moment.

The doorbell rings and my dad gets up from the sofa to answer it. I assume it's our next-door neighbour, as they often pop over on Christmas with some cookies.

A moment later my dad returns to the living room. "Cassidy, it's for you."

For me?

Asher.

I scramble back out from under the table, racing through the living room and into the hallway, not even giving my dad a chance to tell me who it is.

It must be him.

I throw the front door wide open, and it doesn't click till I'm looking at my guest, that my dad knows Asher, loves him and would have invited him in.

But the person standing at the door is definitely not Asher.

It's my other ex-boyfriend. Felix.

Chapter 22

"Felix what are you doing here?" I say angrily, as I step outside, closing the door.

I don't give him time to answer. "And how did you find me?"

Felix rolls his eyes as if I should already know the answer to that question.

"The article. I saw you in the picture with that waste of space, Asher Mills. But I'll forgive that indiscretion. You must have been drunk."

I have no words for him, and he unfortunately continues on. "I'm here to give you the sweeping declaration you wanted, of course. I'm here to take you back." Confusion clouds my voice and thoughts.

"Take me back where?" I ask slowly.

A flash of irritation lights his face, and he says impatiently, as if it's an inconvenience to explain. "Take you back Cassidy. As my girlfriend."

It's so comical I could laugh. Felix it's a very literal, no-nonsense person. He has no time for explanations and lacks more patience than anyone I know.

"Felix… I broke up with you. There's no taking me back if I don't want to be taken anywhere. And I don't. I'm sorry but I didn't ask you to come all this way," I say gently. It's kinder than he deserves. Especially after the way he treated me, and the awful text message I received from him just yesterday.

His expression hardens. "You're being ridiculous Cassidy. We are both engineers. We are married to our jobs. This makes sense. Stop being silly and come home."

Footsteps pound up the stairs, taking my attention off Felix for a moment and my heart skips, before speeding up.

This time, it is Asher.

"I've heard enough. She's repeatedly made it clear that she doesn't want to be with you and she doesn't want you here. And frankly, I don't like the way you are speaking to her. Get out of here before I make you."

My mouth drops open.

Felix crosses his arms and widens his stance, and I have no doubt it's a bluff.

Asher overshadows him by a mile and is very obviously muscled and toned. Unlike Felix.

He laughs but there's a nervous ring to it. "You can't make me do anything. I'll sue you for harassment."

I turn to Felix, my patience worn very thin by now, my kindness of before, all but forgotten.

"I won't let him even touch you Felix, but not to protect you. It's to protect him. You're not worth another second of my time. Please leave now, before I call the police to escort you off my property."

Asher turns to me, raising an eyebrow, followed by a megawatt smile, making my heart skip a beat once more. A warm feeling spreads through my chest and I forget Felix is even here.

"Peaches, I'm impressed." His smile softens and he moves closer to me.

"Look, I need to speak to you. It hasn't even been a full day, but I've missed you so much already. I know you said you wanted some time to think, and I know I should give you all the time you want, and I realise that's selfish and I'm sorry, but also, I'm not sorry. I wanted to chase after you all those years ago and I didn't. This is me chasing now, and I'll chase you forever if that's what I need to do."

His speech is beautiful, but before I can answer him, Felix ruins the moment.

"Oh, you have got to be kidding me. What a joke. You really want this guy? That was the lamest thing I have ever heard." His eyes are narrowed at me, his lips curled in disgust. I'm not quite sure what I even saw in him to begin with.

Asher turns to him, the frustration clear across his face. "You're still here? Haven't we made it clear enough. You aren't wanted here."

Felix opens his mouth to say something, when Asher holds up a hand.

"If I have to pick you up and remove you from the property, I will. Now very kindly, fuck off."

Fear flashes in Felix's eyes and he takes a step back. He looks between both of us, and I hear him swear under his breath. He sneers at me, "You know what. You're not worth it. Good luck, I can't wait to hear how he's left you for a movie star."

Asher growls at him. He freaking growls.

Before he can say or do anything else, Felix hightails it out of here, taking off down the steps and disappearing into the night.

Asher turns back to me, shaking his head. "You were not exaggerating when you said he was a jerk. Who the hell doesn't like Christmas anyway?"

He walks towards me, taking both of my hands. "We've given him too much of our time tonight as it is. Let's forget about him. I know you said you wanted time and if that's still the case I'll leave now and give you that. But this is me chasing you. This is me saying I am all the way in and more. I lost seventeen years with you, and I don't want to waste a second more. You've had my heart all this time and I don't ever want it back."

He takes in a deep breath, before continuing. "I promise I'll protect you as much as I can from the fame, the public, all of it. I've already spoken to my manager, and they have issued a statement to the public and the journalists, paparazzi. Everyone. My private life is mine alone and it's to remain that way. We won't be harassed like that anymore. You, won't be harassed like that ever again and if you are, I will always handle it, Peaches."

I'm overwhelmed by his declarations and the steps he's taken to ensure as much as he can, that I'm safe. That I can continue my life's work, with as little disruption as possible.

It means the world to me.

"Please tell me that you want to be with me. That you want to make this work."

I slip my hands from his and I see his face drop. But only for a moment.

Because in the next moment, I'm taking the last step between us and jumping into his arms, peppering kisses all over his face. He laughs and squeezes me tight, pulling back slightly to search my eyes.

"I take it that's a yes then?"

I laugh, feeling overwhelmingly giddy but in a good way. I feel like I'm twenty-two again, getting a second chance at this.

And my goodness it feels good.

"I love you Asher Mills. And I can promise you that this break was the last one we will ever take."

He plants a soft, open-mouthed kiss on my lips, before lightly biting my lower lip.

"It better be. I'm not letting you go again Cassidy."

"Sounds good to me," I whisper, touching my forehead to his.

I realise then that I didn't even have time to grab a jacket before tearing out here. It's freezing and I shiver, goosebumps covering my arms.

He runs his hands up and down my arms. "You're cold Peaches, let's go."

He takes my hand, kissing my palm. "Where are we going?"

I would go anywhere with him. Even in the middle of a snowstorm.

He kisses the back of my hand. "Not far Peaches," before leading me to my parents' front door.

I glance up at him in surprise.

"Let's go spend Christmas with your family."

He opens the front door, and the heating drifts out, inviting us in.

I lean my head against his arm, letting him lead me down the hallway and into the living room, where we are swarmed, and he is warmly greeted by my family.

This is shaping up to be the best Christmas ever.

He laughs with my mum, before looking for me. He winks at me when he finds me, before turning back to their conversation.

As I look around the room, I see all my favourite people in one place and I send out a silent thanks to The Snowflake Inn, for reconnecting us. The most magical place on Earth.

Epilogue

I STAND STAGE LEFT. WAIT, maybe it's stage right? I can never seem to get that correct.

An excited thrill races through me. I've been waiting for this night for months.

I glance at my watch. Marli is going to be here soon. I haven't seen her in close to seven months and now she is back, after travelling halfway across the world to Australia for her job as a journalist.

It's also, Asher's final concert. At least, for a little while anyway. There are 80,000 screaming fans waiting just past that stage out there, chanting "Ash & Stone", waving glow torches and mobile phones switched to light.

The noise is deafening, and I almost wish I had worn the headphones he suggested I bring.

But there was no way I was tuning any of this out. I'm soaking it all in, riding the wave of anticipation just like everyone else.

It's seriously the coolest thing ever.

Well, other than the fact that just last week, we submitted our artificial kidney project to the regulatory board for approval.

I'm smiling wide just thinking about it, and the impact it's going to have on millions of lives, when a warm arm circles my back, pulling me in close.

I breathe him in, resting my cheek against his chest, still not used to being wrapped up in this gorgeous man's arms. Asher rubs my back as he talks to the stage manager, who is now standing in front of us, running through a set list.

I run my hand up his arm, the lights from the stage catching the diamond on my finger, as it sparkles.

I turn my hand this way and that, loving the sight of my engagement ring.

Seven months after Christmas, Asher and I went back to The Snowflake Inn for Christmas in July, where he asked me to marry him.

It was the easiest yes, I've ever given in my life.

We made a promise to each other then, that we would do everything we could to support each other's careers, and we have done just that.

While it's been challenging at times navigating being away from each other, we are finally in a good rhythm.

In the early days, we would go a few weeks without seeing each other, but now it's a week at the most and usually a few days at best.

Not long after we got engaged, we purchased a home together just twenty minutes from my laboratory. Asher is home whenever he isn't travelling, which is more often these days now that he and the Stone brothers, are spending more time recording in the studio and mentoring new artists.

After seventeen years, of what has seemed like back-to-back concerts, touring and living life in the spotlight, Foster, Kit and Asher decided they wanted to slow down, and they are thriving in their new pace.

Asher laughs, bringing me back to the present, and I stare up at him mesmerised. Everything about him is just so wonderful, and I can't blame his overzealous fans for wanting to know more about the person who stole their favourite rock god's heart. But the truth of it is, we stole each other's heart a long time ago, and we never gave it back.

I've been lucky that the fans have embraced me this year, and I've managed to stay out of the limelight most of the time, despite my fears that it wouldn't be the case.

I shift where I stand, moving my feet to get a little more comfortable.

"Peaches, are you okay?" He stops his conversation immediately, and I can hear the worry in his voice.

I tilt my head back, my smile reassuring.

"I'm fine, I promise. Just a sore back and feet is all. I may have overdone it slightly with standing on my feet all day."

He moves to stand behind me, leaning his head on my shoulder and kissing my cheek, letting me rest back against him, as a contented sigh escapes me. His arms wrap around me, as his hands rest on my growing belly.

"How's our baby girl going in there? Is she hungry?" He kisses my cheek again and I sigh, overjoyed.

I'm in my happy place. I stay in his arms while our baby girl kicks at his hands.

Asher turns me slowly and crouches down, kissing my belly and singing a soft song he wrote for our baby, not caring who is around to see.

I can't wait to watch her face light up when she sees him sing this to her once she's born. I'm five months pregnant, so just over halfway. My plan is to take off a year from work and I cannot wait to take our baby girl to Asher's concerts in the future.

The stage manager races past us again. "You're on in five Asher."

He stands, planting a soft kiss on my lips. "I'm getting you a chair."

I don't even bother telling him no. He won't listen anyway.

He takes off in search of a chair as voices ring out from behind me, ribbing at each other, and I know instantly that it's Foster and Kit Stone. It might be noisy and chaotic back here, but there's no drowning out those two.

They greet me like old friends. I've known the Stone brothers for as long as I've known Asher.

Kit hugs me one armed before taking his bass from the stagehand and moving off to a corner to play some notes, already laser focused on his instrument.

Foster kisses my cheek before gently patting my belly. "How's my niece going in there? I bought her a mini drum set the other day. I can't wait to teach her how to play."

I pat his arm, giving him a warm smile. I've had similar conversations with Kit about the bass too.

This little girl is going to be so spoiled.

"Foster, you're wonderful but I'll tell you what I told Kit. You can keep that at your house, thank you very much."

He grins wide, chuckling. "How about I build you a sound room instead? Can't have my niece being musically deprived."

We are interrupted by a very familiar voice, shouting my name. "Cassidy!"

I turn immediately, tears already springing to my eyes, as I dash towards Marli, throwing my arms around her. We stay like that for a few moments before I reluctantly pull back, wiping my eyes as she does the same.

"I've missed you so much Cass… oh my goodness your belly! It's so cute." She pulls me in for another quick hug before letting me go.

"Argh, that was a nightmare trying to get backstage… oh, ah, hi Foster."

Silence hits the air between us, and I look at them both. Why does this feel weird?

"Umm… you probably don't remember me but I'm Marli. Cassidy's sister. Her twin. We are twins. And sisters."

I narrow my gaze, unsure of what is happening here. Marli is never flustered.

I look between her and Foster, and back again.

This is an interesting development.

His face flushes too and our normally eloquent drummer, is not so eloquent anymore.

"Hi. Marli, hi. I'm… Foster. Wait you just said my name. So, you remember me… I remember you from when Cassidy and Asher dated the first time. Hi."

I've never seen either of them so rattled.

"I… better go find some drumsticks. Seeya!" Foster takes off with a quick wave and Marli groans, covering her face.

"Well, that was uncomfortable." I open my arms, and she walks into them for a hug.

Marli and I have a special bond as twins and not seeing her for such a long time, especially while I was pregnant, was incredibly hard. I'm so excited she is back.

"Umm, so what was that Marli?"

She shrugs, trying to look nonchalant. I see straight through her.

"I had a mega crush on him when you first met Asher and I'm sorry I never told you," she blurts.

I'm stunned into silence. "Okay… I did not expect that at all. So, you've liked him all this time and you never told me?"

She nods sheepishly.

"Well, you know Marli… Foster is single. I'm just saying. And super sweet."

She shakes her head. "I might have a crush, but I can't do sweet. I would eat him alive and then feel bad about it. I need morally grey. Do you have one of those by any chance?"

"Nope, can't say I do. And you don't want one of those outside of our romance books anyway. Trust me."

The stage lights dim and the crowd roars, just as Asher makes his way back to me, chair in hand. I take a moment to appreciate his outfit for tonight. It's really his everyday look most days, but I appreciate it regardless.

His black leather jacket is open, showing his fitted black t-shirt underneath. His jeans are the perfect fit, and his black boots, give him that extra rockstar vibe.

Butterflies dance in my stomach when he gives me that cocky grin of his.

He places the chair down beside me, giving Marli a quick hug before turning his attention back to me, cupping my cheek and planting a soft kiss on my lips.

"I know you won't want to, but the seat is here for you if you need it. Connor is over there if you want anything at all, okay."

Connor waves at me from his spot over by the sound technician and I wave back. The record label insisted Asher have a personal assistant, even though he didn't want one, but he's turned out to be great for him.

"Ash & Stone are on in thirty seconds!" The stage manager calls.

The air is electric, and I'm swept up in the excitement of it all.

A roadie hands Asher his guitar and he takes it, lifting the strap over his head and swinging his guitar to the side.

The crowd seems to have gotten even louder and are now chanting their band name. "Ash & Stone! Ash & Stone!"

Asher leans in close, his lips touching my ear. "I love you, Peaches. Endlessly."

His stagehand moves him towards the edge of the curtain where Kit and Foster stand, and they all run out into the dark, taking their places.

I draw in a deep breath, only releasing it when Marli takes my hand, squeezing it.

"This is so cool Cass. Thank you for inviting me."

The lights turn on, highlighting the three men on stage and the audience cheers, screams echoing through the outdoor stadium.

I've never heard anything like it. Not like it is from up here, on the side of the stage anyway.

Goosebumps prickle my skin and tears well in my eyes. I can't take my eyes off him, a wave of emotion rolling over me at the reality of this being my amazing life.

He strums his guitar once, loudly, eliciting more screams and catcalls from the crowd, before grabbing the mike and walking across the stage like he owns it.

And he does.

Asher Mills is magnetic.

"Good evening, everyone. Thanks for being here tonight. This song is for my beautiful fiancée Cassidy. It's called, 'Snowed Inn'."

Thank you

I hope you enjoyed Cassidy and Asher's story!
I love their love.
MJ xx